POISON PEN

POISON PEN

THE TRUE CONFESSIONS OF TWO TABLOID REPORTERS

Lysa Moskowitz-Mateu
and David LaFontaine

DOVE
B O O K S

ISBN 0-7871-0916-9

Printed in the United States of America

DOVE BOOKS
8955 Beverly Boulevard
Los Angeles, CA 90048
(310) 786-1600

Distributed by Penguin USA

Text design and layout by Stanley S. Drate/Folio Graphics Co. Inc.

First Printing: December 1996

10   9   8   7   6   5   4   3   2   1

CONTENTS

FOREWORD

*O*ne of the first lessons every reporter learns is that the Truth is not a concrete, easily defined–thing. It's not like some bright, shining monolith we can all point at and agree, "Yes, that's the Truth, right there, plain as day." You find out pretty quickly that even with stories as mundane as a car wreck, there are as many Truths as there are people talking. Your job is to try to figure out which one bears the most resemblance to reality.

I realize this is hardly an original observation. In fact, in terms of philosophical acuity, it ranks at about the level of a lame Movie of the Week or ABC Afterschool Special. Anyone who's ever been at the scene of a newsworthy event and then rushed home to watch the replay on the 11 o'clock news, only to wonder if the reporter was watching the same event, could tell you this.

The next lesson every reporter learns is a lot rougher. It comes when you've progressed from simple stenography to more complex stories, when you're chasing a big Truth— one that can really shake things up—through a maze of conflicting stories and self-serving obfuscations.

You find out the Truth costs.

Your sources get fired, or worse, the editor gets angry phone calls or gets roughed up in the parking lot, you get ulcers and your girlfriend dumps you because you're becoming obsessed, and the newspaper's ad manager drinks himself into a coma when a year's contract is pulled.

This book cost, and more than the cover price (but thank you very much anyway—ka-CHING!).

Poison Pen *is unique because it presents an insider's*

view of the tabloid industry, a journey through the surreal-istic world of dumpster-diving, hard-boiled journalistic mis-fits, written from the perspective of two people who were in the thick of our modern, celebrity-obsessed Cult of Per-sonality. In a flamboyant business filled with hundreds of writers dedicated to ferreting out cruel truths, I always wondered why nobody had ever bothered to write a book about the industry itself.

I found out why starting April 23, 1996, when my then-employers at the Star found out about this book and promptly went berserk with suspicion and paranoia.

A bit of background first: The Star and the National En-quirer have both seen their circulations drop to less than 50 percent of what they were only six years ago. Because the Enquirer staff always outnumbered the Star staff by about four to one and were paid at least twice as much, the owners looked to them when it came time to start cutting costs.

So when Mike Walker, the Enquirer's gossip columnist, found out about this book, the Enquirer gleefully seized on it as a reason to point fingers at the Star and claim that the Star herd should be culled, just to save their own miserable hides. Before the final manuscript was even completed, Poison Pen was already the focus of savage corporate trench warfare.

It is a cliché among journalists that although we write about everyone else in every walk of life and expect every-one to have a thick skin and bear up under our very public exposure, we ourselves have the thinnest skin in the world. Reporters and editors react like dyspeptic scorpions to the slightest criticism. But what was really at work, what really turned up the thermostat on me, were the guilty con-sciences of everyone who had spent more than six months wrestling for gobbets of information in the celebrity scan-dal feasting pits that are tabloid newsrooms.

When they heard about this book, everyone I had ever come into contact with felt their stomachs plummeting *further than their morals. I spent more than a week fielding calls from panicked co-workers, all with one question on their minds: "You aren't writing about X . . . are you?" They were all convinced that I had discovered their most shameful peccadilloes and was planning to unmask them. After all, that's what they would do, were the situations reversed.*

They needn't have worried. While a recitation of who knifed whom, who offered what reporter $1,000 just to strip naked, and all the double-dealing, expense-account padding, and outright thievery is somewhat useful in revealing the petty venality of tabloid denizens, narrowing the focus to the misdemeanors of people nobody has heard of would not make an interesting book.

But the Star *didn't believe me. The more I tried to be honest, the more they were convinced I was lying.*

I took a copy of the rough draft of the manuscript to the Star *office and allowed an editor to read through it to prove that I was not out to scuttle anyone's career, that* Poison Pen *was primarily about my and Lysa Moskowitz-Mateu's experiences. All this did was ratchet the fear level up another notch. They knew that I knew where all the bodies are buried and what the toe tags say. The* Star *was convinced that I had "secret chapters" that I was holding back. They were half right.*

Those chapters didn't exist then, but I got right to work on them.

Meanwhile, the threats started rolling in. I was told that the book was a breach of contract and that I would be sued, despite the fact that I had never signed any kind of contract with the Star. *I was told that the book constituted "industrial espionage," that the* Star *was moving to prosecute me, and that I was going to spend the rest of my life in Leavenworth.*

I was barred from the office, and the Star *hired an armed security guard to patrol the premises and shoot me in the head if I tried to clean out my desk. They rummaged through all my notebooks and hired a computer hacker to* break into my computer and try to find anything incriminating they could use against me. A meeting was called of all my co-workers, in which superiors told them that I was the lowest of the low, a thief and a liar, and that if they even dared to talk with me, they would be "fucked." Private investigators were hired to pull everyone's private phone records to find out who had been talking to me, who I was talking to, and who my sources were. The Star was going to bribe Dove not to publish the book; failing that, they were going to assemble a hit team to dig up dirt on publisher Michael Viner and blackmail him into flat-out killing the book.

Then things really got heavy. My seven years of experience watching what happens to people who try to cross the tabs let me know what was coming next. Whenever reporters from Spy or Los Angeles magazine tried to do exposés on the tabloids, they found themselves in the center of a shitstorm of harassment and ultimately buried beneath an ever-mounting pile of legal bills.

It was time to seek legal advice. I was told, "The Star is going to try to crush you like a spider on hot pavement. They not only have to kill your book, but they have to make an example of you, punish you so ferociously that any reporter who even thinks of writing a book like you have will reflexively shit their pants so bad they won't be able to go out in public for a week. If they don't, they face a general uprising, a rebellion. The Star has to crack the whip to keep the other slaves' heads down."

Great.

The next step in my crucifixion was the demand that I bring the manuscript to the main Star offices in New York City. I was told, "You WILL be here tomorrow. With a copy of your book. Period." I knew that the moment I set foot in those offices, my book would be wrenched out of my hands and set before teams of rabid attorneys who would pore over every paragraph, searching for something that would allow them to get an injunction to stop publication. I would *be sued until my gums bled. I would have to move to Alaska and become an elk poacher to escape the constant parade of lawsuits, and still some process server would probably show up at my igloo to garnish my mukluks.*

I didn't have to make that trip.

Perhaps in reaction to this book, but allegedly in reaction to another pending lawsuit, the Star *and* Enquirer *sent a memo to every employee along with an ominously worded sheet of legalese called a confidentiality agreement. Basically, it said that anyone who signed it would not be able to talk about anything they did while at the tabs to anyone for any reason. This despite the fact that we deal with similar forms all the time—celebs use them to try to muzzle their employees—and our standard line is that they aren't worth the paper they're printed on.*

I refused to sign (because I would have been in violation the moment my pen hit paper) and, on May 16, 1996, I was officially fired.

The Truth is such a precious thing that it has to be guarded closely. I guess I still have some of my old journalism-school convictions, beliefs so deeply embedded that not even seven years of cynicism have flayed them out of my soul.

Despite everything, this book is not a personal vendetta against the tabloid industry; in fact, people who have read it have said that, if anything, it portrays tabs and the people who work for them in a mostly favorable way. Yes, there are cold-blooded pit vipers that flourish in this milieu. But you can say that about people in a lot of fields. Arms merchants. Lawyers. Politicians.

In Poison Pen, *Lysa Moskowitz-Mateu, my co-author, fellow reporter, and ex-wife, and I tell it like it is. Lysa worked for four years in the business, first on staff at the* Star *and then freelance. Throughout the book, Lysa's tales are set in roman type. I began my tenure in the tabloid industry in 1989, working also for the* Star. *My escapades are set in italics. Both Lysa and I wanted this book to be a little* more insightful than the standard tell-all, and we hope that among the anecdotes of holing up in four-star hotels and dangling from helicopters, you find some Truth about what tabloids are and why you read them. Because you do. More important, network TV news reads them and then imitates their style and content when bringing you the "News You Can Trust."

Poison Pen *is a portrait of the wild and wicked world of tabloid reporting. It uncovers a facet of the Truth. A Truth that did not come cheap.*

We've attempted to answer the question we've been asked so many times over the years by so many different people: "Where do you guys GET that stuff?"

David LaFontaine
August 1996

POISON
PEN

1

LIVE FAST, DIE YOUNG, AND LEAVE A GOOD-LOOKING CORPSE

River Phoenix was pronounced dead at 1:51 A.M. on Monday, November 1, 1993. Until that time, I had been going about my life reporting for the tabloids, trying my best to make a living at something I inherently despised. The news of his death came after I'd been out much of the night, celebrating Halloween. I awoke to the voice of *Star* bureau chief Bob Smith on my answering machine, saying that River Phoenix had died and that he wanted me to work on the story. The casual way he relayed the information was strange. His voice was flat and completely devoid of emotion. Yet that wasn't unusual for Bob or for most other tabloid reporters and editors, who tend to approach the news from a detached, stoic point of view. Indifference seems to be a prerequisite for the job.

But for me, hearing the news of River's death was like being blind-sided. Not only was I a fan of his, but he was too young, too talented to die. I immediately knew I'd be unable to cover the story dispassionately. I drove to the Viper Room, the nightclub where River spent his last hours. For a long while I sat with the mourners who had

come to pay their respects, watching reporter after reporter come by the scene, which had turned into a memorial covered with cards, flowers, candles, and posters
of River's films. I didn't speak to anyone. I was too over-
wrought.

I later wrote and filed the story, but something had
shifted inside of me. Sensationalizing such tragedy and invading people's private lives at such private times had become too much to bear, and I knew my career as a tabloid
reporter would soon be over. Two years later, it was.

It's not unusual for most people to have an inordinate
fascination with the tabloids and the celebrities who grace
their pages. Over the four years I worked for the tabs, trav-
eling around the country on breaking stories, people everywhere would ask me endless questions about the business,
anxious to hear all the dirt on their favorite stars. I came to
realize that there was not only a vast market for a book
about the tabloid industry, but also an even greater need
for me and veteran tab reporter and co-author David La-
Fontaine to tell the truth about what really goes on behind
closed doors. After all, our jobs gave us insight into the
human mind: how far people will go to make a buck, and
how ludicrous amounts of money are thrown around to
land a breaking story.

Working for the tabloids had never been a lifelong
dream for either David or me. Having penned my first book
at the age of eleven, I wanted to pursue a career in writing
and had a simultaneous interest in the world of Hollywood.
David ended up at the tabloids after coming to Los Angeles
only to encounter a hiring freeze at the newspaper that had
promised him a job.

David and I had something in common with a lot of tab
reporters, though: We had the ability to write, the balls to
do crazy shit, and the need for constant thrills and stimula-
tion. Although our backgrounds and personalities are very
different, we shared similar experiences and frustrations
working in the rag business.

Most people think of tabloid reporters as sleazy and immoral, with nothing better to do than spy on celebrities and expose their lives. Perhaps they think of us as capable only of living vicariously through the rich and famous and never stopping to think about the impact our words might have on those we write about. But David and I are not your typical tab reporters. Although we've had fun peeking into the life of a celebrity, on the down side we've spent sleepless nights realizing that that celebrity's painful divorce would be next week's news and that someone's death, illness, or tale of infidelity was just another story.

My career in the tabloids began at the *Star* on December 15, 1991. I had read the *Star* since I was a teenager and thought there was nothing wrong with the magazine's forthright way of dishing up dirt. I never thought that someday I'd be the one writing the smut.

The way I got the job was a stroke of luck. Two weeks after moving back to Los Angeles from New York City, I was jobless and sitting in my apartment, flipping through the *Star*, when I spotted the following ad: "If you have access to accurate Hollywood gossip and want to make extra money, call our Los Angeles office."

I dialed the number. The woman who answered told me to send in my resumé and clippings, which I promptly did. Two days later I received a call from L.A. bureau chief Bob Smith. Bob hails from Scotland and has a heavy accent, so I hardly understood a word he said. After deciphering "interview" and "tomorrow," I hung up feeling ecstatic and surprised. Although I'd been a writer for some time and had had articles published in various spiritual and art magazines, I had never written anything remotely related to celebrity trash. (That shows how much of a journalism background you need in order to get a job with the tabloids.)

Walking into the *Star* office that first time was quite a trip. Candid pictures of celebrities such as Hugh Hefner, Elizabeth Taylor, and Michael Jackson covered the walls of the tiny reception area. Back issues of the magazine were piled up next to the couch. Bob turned out to be a rather cartoonish, stocky man with gray hair, short fingers, and a long mustache. After the first five minutes of the interview, I was hired. I would be working three days a week to start, at $120 a day. I was thrilled. I had never made that kind of money before in my life.

I came to work the following Monday at 9 A.M. sharp and was surprised to see that no one but the secretary was there. Despite being ruthless and competitive, tabloid reporters are also a notoriously lazy bunch, always coming in late or ideally not at all. I was later introduced to the other reporters, who were an eclectic mix of Brits, "real" newspaper wanna-be's, and veteran tab reporters.

I remember my first assignment vividly. I had been sent to Ventura County to interview a psychic who ran a dating service. She had supposedly set up many successful dates that turned into marriages. My mission was to get the inside scoop. I quickly discovered that the successful psychic was not successful at all: Of her clients, only two out of a hundred had gotten married. Not exactly a brilliant track record. I returned to the office with a lame story. Bob told me to write up what I had.

I had no idea how to write a tabloid article. I didn't know you needed a punchy lead and a snappy ending to tie the story together. I didn't know how to structure the story or label sources.

So I faked it.

The second story I was assigned involved Donny Osmond cheating on his wife with actress Crystal Bernard of TV's "Wings." A woman had called in claiming she had proof that Donny and Crystal were fooling around. She had seen them kissing and hugging on the set of a film Crystal was shooting, on the set of "Wings," and on several other occasions. By tabloid standards, the woman was giving us no proof at all. Proof consists of a photo, a love letter, or anything tangible that will hold up in court. Merely saying that a husband is cheating on his wife isn't enough.

I spent hours on the phone with this source, grilling her for every intricate detail about Donny and Crystal. I asked her to meet me at a restaurant, but she refused. I talked to Bob and expressed my doubts about the accuracy of the woman's claims. The *Star* decided to run the story on the cover anyway. They pasted Donny's picture next to Crystal in a pose suggesting they were intimately involved.

I was a quick study in this business of deceit. I learned how to write catchy leads, how to exaggerate the truth, and how to con my way into film premieres and other Hollywood events. By saying I was a casting agent or that I worked for a film studio, I could get free tickets and get on the guest list for private parties. In the tabloid industry, being a good liar is considered a highly desirable trait.

The business is extremely addictive: We reporters live for the next big scoop. We live for the rush that comes when the bureau chief tells us to pack our things and get to the airport in less than an hour to catch a plane to Cancun or New York. Sometimes all we're told is to catch a plane.

Although working for the tabloids is quite a ride for anyone, both David's and my situation was complicated because of our relationship. David and I met at the *Star* in 1991, shortly after I was hired, and within four months we moved in together. I quit the *Star* in December 1992. In April 1994 we were married.

Until I quit, David and I freely and openly gave each other leads and worked on stories together. After I left and began freelancing for the *National Enquirer* and the *Globe*, that practice continued, but in secret. The *Enquirer* and the *Globe* wouldn't hire me on staff because of my relationship with David. They felt it was too risky to have two cohabiting reporters working for competing magazines.

During the year we worked at the *Star*, David and I traveled all over the United States. It was an exciting time, and we would often talk about how we couldn't have done the

things we did and seen the things we saw if we didn't work
for the tabloids. David and I lived the life that the people
we were chasing lived. We ate at the same restaurants,
stayed at the same posh hotels—the Bel Air, the Peninsula,
and Ma Maison Sofitel, to name a few—and spent the same
amount of money. The difference was that the celebrities'
money was their own, whereas ours was provided by the
Star.

Ultimately, though, invading the lives of the rich and famous by posing as one of them just didn't feel right. It's like
the line Billy Crystal says to Meg Ryan in the film *When
Harry Met Sally*, after she assures him that her future is
to go to journalism school and become a reporter. Crystal
sardonically replies, "So you can write about things that
happen to other people?"

Such is the story of our lives.

Love in the Time of Tabloids

*Love in the tabloid world is a treacherous thing. Living
with and marrying Lysa cost me a tremendous amount of
credibility, of opportunity, of respect from my co-workers
and even from my competitors. Some of the wounds were
self-inflicted because I didn't yet understand how an open
alliance between two people working in such an inherently
clandestine industry would be viewed.*

*But a lot of the grief I took was the result of cutlery
aimed at my dorsal region. When the other reporters in the
office were working on hot stories and wanted to discuss
them among themselves, they always left the newsroom because they were sure I would leak them to Lysa. When good
assignments came up, Bob gave them to someone else so
Lysa wouldn't hear about them. The only stories I worked
on were the ones I was able to generate on my own.*

*Meanwhile, the tales of our office romance grew in
the telling. At various times, we were supposedly caught
having sex in the stairwell, in my car in the underground*

parking lot, in the office kitchen, and on my desk after hours. Everyone assumed that when I left the office to go on a stakeout, I was really going to meet Lysa and blow off work. I was labeled lazy and insubordinate and all those whom Lysa had alienated (which was almost everyone in the office) took every chance they could to glue that label tighter on me.

The reality of the situation was that I was doing good work despite all the distractions and backbiting, churning out cover stories and gossip items, working every weekend, and going out of town on assignment with no notice. I was still faithfully making sacrifices to the imperatives of the Star.

Everything came to the boiling point, though, when I was nailing down a story on David Carradine's daughter, Calista, who had been arrested for prostitution in Seattle. Not only did I have to deal with a squirrelly source who had an axe to grind and a long criminal record, but I also had the Brits nipping at my heels. Turned out another reporter in the office had stolen my source's phone number off my desk and fed it to a confederate at the London Sun, who then called my source and tried to steal him away from me. Things grew more complicated as the source played us off each other, trying to get us to bid the price up. He refused to give me crucial bits of information until he got a signed contract, because the guy at the Sun kept telling him I was going to screw him over.

In spite of all this, I got the full story, along with photos of Calista Carradine standing in the hallway of the courthouse, even though no cameras were allowed. I returned to the L.A. office expecting a pat on the head or at least some kind of recognition for a job well done under trying circumstances.

Silly boy.

Instead, I was called into a closed-door meeting in Bob Smith's office and told that the story was a monumental fuck-up, that I was a sullen and rebellious employee who *didn't get along with the others, and that if my "attitude" didn't improve, I would be fired. I felt like I had wandered into a Kafka novel. Every mistake I made was magnified into an earth-shattering blunder, while everything that turned out well was minimized and sneered at. The real issue, of course, was my relationship with Lysa and how I had become "worthless and distracted" ever since I started dating her. But I didn't stop.*

It wasn't until Lysa pretty much wore out her welcome at the Globe *and* Enquirer *that the situation improved. When she came back to work for the* Star, *they could no longer accuse me of feeding her info to use at the other magazines. Which did not mean I wasn't feeding her info to use at the* Star.

When my sources would call with a good lead, I would sometimes pass it to Lysa. It made perfect sense at the time: My sources were giving me more than I could handle, and Lysa could use the $750 to $1,500 per article to pay her bills. When she came up with a story on her own, I would use my knowledge and sources to help her fill in the blanks and add crucial anecdotes to make the story marketable.

Even though we divorced in 1995, Lysa continued to make money this way. In one conversation, I let slip what I knew about Matthew Perry and Julia Roberts moving in together. From that, Lysa was able to concoct a story claiming that Julia wanted to have Matthew's baby. An utterly safe story to make up out of thin air, because as long as you know they are actually living together, you can safely assume that they've talked about children. No jury would find any cause to uphold a libel suit filed on the basis of "the Star *said Julia was really in love with the man she was living with at the time and wanted to bear his kids."*

This basic practice of taking a tiny seed of fact and subjecting it to tabloid radiation until it mutates into an alien plant supports a legion of freelance writers. Tabloid news is now a worldwide industry, which means that a sharp freelancer can sell the same story three or four times *minimum, depending on how prominent the celebrity involved is. The current champs are the Australian magazines, because they pay top dollar for any kind of exclusive scoop. A story that would bring $500 in the United States can sell for $3,000 or more "down under," especially if the reporter can come up with a photo.*

Next in line are London's fabled Fleet Street newspapers, the breeding ground for most of the tabloid journalists at work in the United States today. The Brits love juicy scandals, and they're not afraid to go for the throat. They'll print explicit, blow-by-blow (ahem) accounts of illicit sexual dalliances, drug orgies, health problems, whatever they can get their hands on. They love topless shots of bimbos telling all about their low-rent rendezvous with married Hollywood actors.

Finally, there are the Germans, French, Italians, Spanish, and Scandinavians, whose interest in TV and movie stars is unpredictable. For example, when I worked the David Hasselhoff wedding, the paparazzi were in an absolute frenzy. They broke into an apartment building bordering the Little Brown Church on Coldwater Canyon Avenue and were hanging over the railing while fending off the screaming landlady. Why? Hasselhoff is Germany's national hero, with the top-rated TV show and a string of number one albums. Magazines such as Bild Zeitung *and* Der Spiegel *were offering $50,000 for a good picture of him and his new bride.*

French photographers have made enough to retire on the Cap d'Antibes by just hanging around Princess Stephanie's house in Burbank, shooting pictures of her doing anything—*walking her dog, doing the laundry, scratching her butt*—*and selling the shots for big bucks to* Voici, Paris Match, *and* Oggi.

The whole tabloid business now operates by under-the-table graft. Suppose a lead comes in that Stallone is going to be riding horses with his latest girlfriend somewhere in Malibu. At one time, the normal, and honest, chain of *events would have the reporter picking up the phone, calling the photo desk, and assigning a photographer. The photographer would get the details from the reporter, go out and shoot the pictures, and the magazine would get the shot for only the $250 day rate they paid to the lensperson.*

Nowadays, the reporter still calls up the photographer, who goes out and shoots the pictures. But then the photographer offers to sell the picture to the magazine for thousands of dollars, and flogs it to publications around the world for even more money. The reporter writes a story to go with the photo and pays her or his source just enough to keep the source happy. The photographer splits with the reporter whatever money he or she makes. A single story and photo can net a double-dealer anywhere from $3,000 to $30,000, depending on how hot the picture is and what kind of story the reporter can concoct to sell it.

Some risky business. Read on, and you'll learn more about its inner workings and the love-hate relationship Lysa and I had with it. In the next chapter, you'll get a rundown of the evolution of tabloid magazines, as well as more than a few insights into just why so much of America is fascinated by the tabs.

2

TRUTH, PROBABILITIES, POSSIBILITIES, AND LIES, OR: A BRIEF HISTORY OF SLIME

> Journalists are as disruptive a menace to the public body as stones in the gall bladder are to the private body. They are the scavengers of society, who, possessing no guts of their own, tear out the guts of celebrities.
> —*Dylan Thomas*

> The American press, with very few exceptions, is a kept press. Kept by the big corporations the way a whore is kept by a rich man.
> —*Theodore Dreiser*

*I*n 1989, I arrived in Los Angeles with $600 and a suitcase, fresh from the Caracas Daily Journal, where I had worked as a reporter, news editor, and managing editor. During my time there, I interviewed presidents, world leaders, and guerrillas alike, and contributed to important investigative pieces that helped shape the destiny of an entire country. I was headed for the States primed to apply these same investigative skills to an American newspaper, The Orange County Register, which had offered me a job. Unfortunately, my arrival coincided with the economy going into the toilet and a hiring freeze in the newspaper industry.

I wound up at Star *magazine.*

At the time, the tabloid world was contemptuously scorned and disregarded. Tabloids were thought of as a sick joke, good only for the occasional Bigfoot or UFO story. No self-respecting journalist would even admit to reading them, except to get a cheap laugh while standing in the checkout line at the grocery store.

Now, seven years later, I find my stories quoted in the Los Angeles Times *and* Time *magazine and followed up on by TV newsmagazine shows. I have had reporters who covered the O.J. Simpson trial bug me for quotes and beg me to tip them off whenever I get a hot scoop.*

The stories the tabloids break are ripped off by main-stream newspapers and magazines, which proceed to write about how horribly certain celebs have been treated by the tabs, then fill the rest of the article by gleefully repeating all the dirt word for word. Meanwhile, TV talk shows have posted huge ratings gains by hyping tabloid-type stories. And let's not forget that for more than a year, national newscasts were dominated by a story that was and is, at its core, pure tabloid: the Simpson trial.

America has turned tabloid.

How did we get here?

There is no simple answer. A complicated mix of social factors, economic woes, and political pressures has brought this facet of pop culture into the spotlight.

First of all, despite the popular perception that the tabs burst onto the scene only in the last few years, their particular style of news is actually centuries old, perhaps as old as humanity.

It's gossip.

Sometimes it's mean-spirited, as in a last kick in the ribs to a troubled, fallen celeb checking into rehab. Sometimes it's sympathetic, as in a paean to a beloved star dying of cancer. Sometimes it's well-deserved, as in taking an arrogant young punk down a few notches. If a Pulitzer-winning news story is a Mona Lisa of subtle shadings, muted tones, and photorealistic detail, a tabloid story is a screaming, psychedelic, Day-Glo, in-your-face piece of pop art. In tabloid stories, everything is presented as its absolute extreme. There are no gray areas. It's almost operatic: shining good guys, skulking bad guys, flaming red anger, sickly green jealousy, heartache, and redemption.

This type of news has been popular in America since we were a British colony. Pamphleteers and scandal sheets were integral to the American Revolution, although the penalties back then involved nooses and gallows rather than libel suits and court orders. George Washington and Thomas Jefferson were mocked and slandered mercilessly in ways that would get modern-day political reporters suspended or fired.

Jefferson, who initially said that he preferred a free press to a strong government, later became so disgusted by the vitriolic attacks leveled at him that he suggested editors divide their newspapers into four sections: Truth, Probabilities, Possibilities, and Lies. "The newspapers of our country, by their abandoned spirit of falsehood, have more effectively destroyed the utility of the press than all the shackles devised by Bonaparte," he once said in despair.

Mark Twain captured the rough, brawling style of journalism in the mid-1800s with his scathing stories, back when anyone who could scrape together a few bucks could buy a printing press and become a publisher. On an average day, the owner/editor/reporter slandered every prominent citizen in town, taunted and ridiculed everyone who disagreed with him, and was consequently shot, stabbed, beaten by an angry mob, and tarred and feathered, then had his business burned to the ground.

These days they sic lawyers on us.

By the early 1900s, newspapers had evolved into huge, powerful organizations with staffs of hundreds of reporters, artists, and photographers spread all over the globe. This was the start of the circulation wars. It is the essential arithmetic of journalism: the more people who read the *paper, the more money you make. How do you get people to read? Simple. Tell better stories. It soon becomes a game of "Can You Top This?"*

In New York City, newspaper barons Joseph Pulitzer (yes, as in the prize) and William Randolph Hearst went head to head every day to get the wildest stories and get them first. A favorite cartoon character at the time was The Yellow Kid, used in advertisements to try to get readers to buy the New York Journal. *Hence the phrase* yellow journalism, *which refers to the style of sensationalistic, screaming headlines and exaggerated copy.*

How far would these moguls go to sell papers? The Spanish-American War of 1898 was a direct result of the circulation battles. The papers seized on the plight of the Cubans, who were ruled by Spain. Day after day, they reported on the appalling conditions under which poor, ragged, starving Cubans were bound into slavery and worked to death in the fields and mines by their cruel Spanish masters, who whipped them for disobedience and hung them for trying to escape. Cuba was portrayed as a virtual death camp.

Problem was, none of it was true.

The editorial pages harangued the U.S. government to go to war and free the Cubans. Hearst sent artist Frederic Remington to Cuba to do some sketches. He arrived before the U.S. battleship Maine *exploded and sank, and so he found nothing. Remington, who is perhaps best known for his sketches and sculptures of cowboys and bucking broncos, got bored and asked to come back.* "EVERYTHING IS QUIET. THERE IS NO TROUBLE HERE. THERE WILL BE NO WAR. I WISH TO RETURN," *he telegraphed. Hearst shot back his reply:* "PLEASE REMAIN. YOU FURNISH THE PICTURES AND I'LL FURNISH THE WAR."

And Hearst did. Bowing to public pressure, which had been whipped into a frenzy by the papers, particularly after the sinking of the Maine, *the United States declared war on Spain. American troops slaughtered Spain's ill-equipped soldiers, sank their antiquated navy, and took possession of Cuba, the Philippines, and other territories. Disgusted by the travesty, Pulitzer reined in his papers' coverage and tried to take the high road from then on. In other words, he ordered his reporters and editors to start printing the truth again.*

The next big evolutionary step took place in the 1920s, and has been labeled jazz-age journalism. Photography was the newest development, and the New York Mirror, *the* New York Daily News, *and the* Evening Graphic *took full advantage of it, printing grisly shots of accidents, crime scenes, and disasters. Eager photographers—predecessors of today's paparazzi—carried all kinds of props. They carted buckets of water in the trunks of their cars, which they would splash around the bodies of Mob victims. On black-and-white film, lit by the searing glare of the flash-bulbs, the water on the pavement looked just like pools of blood. One photographer was famous for carrying around a pair of baby shoes, which he would strategically place amid the ruins of a tenement fire or church collapse to make the disaster that much more poignant.*

In 1928, Tom Howard, a Daily News *photographer, arranged to be a witness at the execution of Ruth Snyder, who had been convicted of murdering her husband. As he waited, he put his foot up on a table, casually leaned on his knee, and slightly lifted his trouser leg. When the switch was thrown, he snapped a picture using a camera strapped to his ankle. It was hyped as the first Sing Sing execution photo and the first of a woman's execution. The* Daily News *ran the shot full-page, pointing out gleefully that Snyder's hand was blurry because the current was making her body twitch and convulse. That issue sold 250,000 copies; 750,000 more were later printed and sold.*

Pretty strong meat for those more genteel times.

If the papers didn't have a picture, they resorted to a trick still in use today: the Composmograph, a photo that has been enhanced, altered, or posed. The Evening Graphic *used it to create such images as the king of England in his bathtub, a naked showgirl bathing in champagne as a Broadway producer looked on, and Enrico Caruso show-ing Rudolph Valentino the sights in heaven. For its efforts, the* Graphic *was quickly nicknamed "the Porno-Graphic."*

Modern-day tabloids use computer imaging and celeb-rity look-alikes on their covers. The Star *has run shots of an ersatz Liz Taylor reclining in Michael Jackson's hyperbaric chamber and a doughy Roseanne doppelgänger throwing her wedding bouquet. Then there are the shots of Oprah Winfrey's head on someone else's body, Elvis Presley as he would look today, and space aliens pounding the gavel in the opening session of Congress.*

Chicago had about a half dozen fiercely competing daily newspapers in the 1920s, and each one sent its reporters out on kamikaze missions. Just like in the movie The Front Page, *reporters would break any law, tell any lie, to get the scoop. The Hildy Johnson immortalized in that film really existed. He would do things like impersonate a prison guard and kidnap a murderer to interview him, and steal a human stomach from the morgue to be photographed and analyzed in a poisoning case. He also paid $200 for an ex-clusive interview with a killer on death row, then won the money back in a card game. "Don't play rummy with Hildy Johnson," the prisoner told the priest on the way to the electric chair. "I think he cheats."*

By the 1950s, the last element in the making of the mod-ern tabloid fell into place: relentless coverage of Hollywood celebrities. Confidential *magazine, the Cro-Magnon of tab-loids, rose up and began hunting down its prey by giving bribes to hookers and drug dealers and using ambush pho-tography on stars leaving sleazy bars and no-tell motels. The magazine grew so powerful that the studios themselves started cutting deals. In return for killing embarrassing sto-ries about big stars like Rock Hudson, the studio weasels would tip off the tabloid to the indiscretions of smaller stars* and allow them to be trapped, photographed, written up, and sold down the river.

After the demise of Confidential, tabloid-style reporting went into a dormant period as the tide of popular culture turned toward Vietnam and later Watergate. Enter Generoso Pope, a hell-bent-for-leather eccentric publisher who dreamed of one day owning a tabloid that would attract 20 million readers. He bought a wheezing weekly called the New York Enquirer in 1952, and by the 1970s it was the National Enquirer, full of sex, sleaze, and space aliens.

It was Pope who hit upon the idea of placing tabloids and other magazines in the checkout lines of supermarkets. Pope was also friendly with some rather unpleasant people who, it was said, ran the New York crime syndicates commonly known as the Mafia. It is more than hearsay that those friendships had a great deal to do with Pope's outstanding success at getting supermarket owners to ditch the razor blades and candy bars in favor of the Enquirer. ("Ya' gotta' nice store here. Be a shame if something were to happen . . .")

Pope boosted the Enquirer's circulation from 17,000 to close to five million. He read every single word that went into the paper and worked long hours in the office, sometimes wearing only swim trunks and slippers. A throwback to the old press barons Hearst and Pulitzer, Pope cared intensely about the stories that went into his baby, and nothing would stand in his way once he made up his mind.

Another twentieth-century mogul is much the same way: Rupert Murdoch, one of the richest men in the world, with a communications/entertainment conglomerate that spans the globe. Murdoch founded the Star in the seventies to compete with the Enquirer, bringing to it his brash Aussie style and go-for-the-throat journalistic instincts. Not long after, the Star's circulation was just a few hundred thousand less than the Enquirer's circulation.

That was when the British invasion began. Pope and Murdoch started offering high salaries to writers who *could stomach the down-and-dirty kind of reporting they were looking for. And London's Fleet Street reporters, who are to this day far more vicious and ruthless than U.S. tab reporters, flocked over in droves.*

As Peter Kent, a reporter for the Star, *put it, "There you are in London, freezing your arse off half the year, the other half it's pissing down rain. You're living in a dreary flat downwind of smokestacks belching soot into the air, covering the Irish troubles and getting shot at every day. And you're getting paid shit.*

"Then along comes some crazy Yank who offers to triple your salary and moves you to Miami, where it's sunny and warm all the time, and you can buy a house and screw beautiful thong-bikini women with big tits while drinking frothy cocktails with little umbrellas and plastic monkeys on the side. Who wouldn't jump at that?"

By the mid-1980s, virtually every high-level executive, along with numerous editors and reporters, was a former Fleet Streeter. Their experience in relentlessly pursuing Britain's royal family was perfect training for their new jobs pursuing America's version of royalty: celebrities.

Exposing the Glass Teat

It is no accident that the phenomenal growth of the tabloids and tabloid-style news has coincided with the American public's seemingly bottomless appetite for intimate details of the private lives of the celebrities they worship. All the stories about forbidden love triangles and treacherous domestic murder plots still get a lot of ink (another helping of Buttafuoco, anyone?), but what really sells are the crime, slime, and the somebody-done-somebody-wrong songs involving a celebrity. To get to the reason why, we must first cut right to the heart of what journalists consider news.

A cynical definition of news is "bad stuff happening to other people." I really can't argue too strongly against this viewpoint. After all, it's one of the foundations of any newspaper or broadcast: that little thrill we get reading about or seeing dramatic shots of victims wandering through tornado-ravaged trailer parks or leaping from blazing high-rise apartment buildings.

We are fascinated with death and disaster. We want it presented just close enough so that we can see every detail, yet at arm's length so that we can escape untouched. We feel superior to the victims. We feel lucky. We briefly imagine ourselves in that situation, and it jolts us out of our humdrum, everyday rut.

And then we flip to the next channel.

The classic definition of news is encapsulated in a quotation from New York Sun *editor John Bogart: "When a dog bites a man, that is not news. When a man bites a dog, that's news." Basically, anything out of the ordinary is news.*

A more high-minded and noble definition was given by Lord Northcliff, owner of the Times *of London, who said news is "what somebody somewhere wants to suppress. All the rest is advertising."*

But these definitions do not explain why the tabloids have had such success with stories about celebrities. And that's because they don't take into account the biggest sociological force of the twentieth century: television.

I first saw what a force television was in American society when, ironically, I was no longer in American society. As a news editor in Caracas, Venezuela, it was my job to pick and choose the most important stories of the day to go on the front page for the large expatriate population. During the 1988 U.S. presidential campaign, I started to notice that stories that seemed silly and insignificant were getting huge play on the wire services; for example, the story about how dorky Michael Dukakis looked riding around in a tank in an attempt to toughen his image. At about the same time, the savings and loan crisis was climaxing, the federal deficit was growing, and relations with the collapsing Soviet Union had to be rethought.

And yet both the AP and UPI devoted story after story to

Dukakis in that tank. When I looked more closely at the photos, I realized why. They had that grainy, horizontal-line look of transferred video images.

This was a TV story.

It wasn't the most important story, not by a long shot. But it was the story that looked best on TV, and thus it led the nightly TV news broadcasts.

Not so long ago, people in the newspaper industry complained that all TV news did was "read the paper over the air," because newspapers had the staff and the know-how and were the ones breaking stories. Such is no longer the case.

So this is the definition we're left with: What's news is whatever's on TV. Television has fused America—a country founded by wild-eyed individualists and settled by the non-conformist dregs of every other self-respecting country—into a single culture more effectively than any fascistic propagandist's dream. At one time, a rural Southerner and a Rust Belt Midwesterner had totally different heroes and mind-sets. These days, you're likely to find both of them speaking in a faux surfer accent idolizing MTV's Buzz Clip Hero of the Month. Television provides us with our cultural frame of reference. No matter where I've traveled in the United States, I can stop in at any diner and have a conversation with the locals about Roseanne or O.J.

This is not meant to be yet another tiresome indictment of the amount of time Americans spend vegetating in front of what author Harlan Ellison called "The Glass Teat." It is just a statement of fact that our collective reality now is whatever we see on television. Inasmuch as that binds us together as a culture, it profoundly isolates us as individuals. In the old days, the men gathered at the barber shop and the women at the beauty salon to chew over the latest town gossip. Unfortunately, that's not really possible nowadays, when everyone is from different social groupings and economic strata. But there is one class of people that we're all familiar with and interested in.

Celebrities.

We all know them because they are shoved into our faces every night through our one common experience: watching TV. On their TV shows, in their promos for their movies, in their sneaker ads, whatever, we see their larger-than-life image, and from those we form images about their personalities and private lives. Madonna is a nasty temptress who devours men. Arnold Schwarzenegger is an implacable success machine with the right quip for every occasion. Lucille Ball was a goofy but devoted family woman as well as a successful businesswoman. Because we see these people in our homes, we feel a real connection with them. That's why we watch their shows, buy their sneakers, listen to their records.

And so, when we get in the elevator and the doors close and there's that awkward moment of silence, the safe topic, a sure icebreaker, is the latest O.J. joke. Or Hugh Grant joke.

This is where the tabloids come in. We supply you all with the gossip that would otherwise be missing. Tabloids are the $1.29 supermarket checkout line equivalent of the overweight old harridan leaning over the back fence, wagging her finger and clucking about people who should know better.

An old journalism professor of mine taught me that the key to selling your work was to know your market and tailor your story to fit what the magazines want. The tabloids have to tailor their content to the readers, or else the readers don't read anymore, and pretty soon there's office space for rent.

Well, who reads the tabloids? People who watch a lot of TV and like to gossip. Homemakers. Retired people. People without a lot of disposable income to go out and amuse themselves in other ways. People who, by and large, have a pretty gritty time making it from one day to the next. People who generally don't have advanced degrees from prestigious universities. These people want to read about the lifestyles of the rich and famous, about vacations in exotic places they will never visit, about expensive gourmet dinners they will never get to taste, about dancing the night away in clubs that would never let them through the front door.

But they want it all presented to them a certain way. And herein lies the key, the Secret Message of the Tabloids: The readers want to be told that despite being young, beautiful, and rich and famous, the celebrities they read about are just as miserable as they are.

The problem with this secret message is that it simply isn't true. Hate to spoil your cherished illusions, but by and large, celebrities are having a hell of a lot more fun than you ever will. Case in point: Jack Nicholson. Jack got $50 million for Batman and has maybe ten times that in his portfolio. He's not worrying about making the payment on the Hyundai. Jack lives in a $10 million estate atop the Hollywood Hills, filled with priceless works of art. He's instantly catered to and given the best seats in the house wherever he goes. And he has the most beautiful women in the world lining up, begging to have kinky sex with him every spare second of the day.

But is he really happy? Doesn't he get upset when he has to read those cruel stories about his drunken debauchery?

C'mon. Get serious. You couldn't wipe the smile off Jack's face with TNT.

All this garbage about poor little rich celebrities being prisoners of their fame, about wishing they could be just ''normal folks'' so they could do their grocery shopping in peace, is a giant load of shit.

Don't believe me? Fine. Ask Demi Moore if she'll trade the beach house in Malibu, the limos and Learjets, the premieres and precious stones, for a dead-end, soul-killing job in a plastic-extrusion factory, married to a fat, sweaty slob who ignores her and falls asleep on the couch every night. See how far you get.

This image of loneliness and heartache at the top is one

of the great myths of the twentieth century. Anyone who wants to get off the big merry-go-round of fame can bail out if he or she really wants to. The tabloids just keep pounding away at this message because it's the one the readers want to hear.

Who knows? Maybe foisting this secret message on the American people is a good thing. Maybe the belief that we're all miserable together, that we all have our crosses to bear, is what keeps the have-nots from pouring over the gates and fences like a tide. Look at the 1995 Oklahoma City bombing, in which your basic losers took out their frustration at being trapped in a society where they felt rewards were denied them. The L.A. riots of 1992 were viewed as a violent upwelling of anger over police injustice but more of a free shopping spree for people who had never had nice things. Things like you see the people on TV having.

And what was the most-often looted item? Television sets, of course.

Then again, maybe having tabloids serve as a vent for have-not envy isn't such a good thing in the long run. Statistics show that the disparity between the classes is becoming more and more marked with each passing year. Maybe we do need another American Revolution to overturn the taxation without representation, to rework the mechanisms that are supposed to introduce some sort of equity in the distribution of wealth.

If that's really the case, well, we're all in a hell of a lot more trouble than a few tabloids could generate, anyway.

It's obvious that when the attention of the country is focused on tabloid-style news, it sure isn't focused on the real news. Real problems that need real solutions fall by the wayside as the national discourse centers around a barking Akita named Kato or Hugh Grant's bargain-basement rendezvous with a whore.

I hear the same excuses from Generation Xers and others who should know better: "After a hard day at work, I just want to zone out." "Why do I need to find Bosnia on a map, anyway?" "I've got so many important things screaming for my attention that I just want to hear about something light, something funny."

And so they pick up the Star, *tune into "Entertainment Tonight," and watch "The Gossip Show" on E!*

Tabloid news is Twinkies for the brain. It's soft and mushy, gives you a sweet rush, and has no real substance. And the first thing you want to do after you're done is scarf down another. There's nothing wrong with having a Twinkie once in a while. But a steady diet of them will rot your brain right out of your head.

3

EVERY BREATH YOU TAKE . . .

Stalkers Abound
Los Angeles, California
Spring 1992

W hen Janet Jackson was being stalked, she was terrified that the deranged man, who had professed his everlasting love for her, would snap and do something violent. She was sure he was capable of it, so she took precautions. She hired four security guards and three burly bodyguards to protect her while she was filming *Poetic Justice* in the spring of 1992. The bodyguards followed her every move around the set, and the security guards were stationed in their vehicles along the perimeter of Griffith Park, where the film was being shot. Both sets of guards were in constant contact via walkie-talkie.

A lewd and twisted soul who was deluded into believing he was her husband, the stalker wrote more than fifty perverted letters a week and made vulgar phone calls to Janet's house on a regular basis. What made the situation more frightening was the fact that Janet didn't know who the obsessed man was, what he looked like, or when he would strike again.

Stalker stories are always creepy, especially for reporters. One never knows how far an obsessed fan will go in order to get closer to the object of their "affection." There have been times in David's career when a stalker ended up becoming obsessed with *him.*

By probing too far into the secret world of the stalker, David has sometimes been rewarded with vile phone calls in the middle of the night or a Peeping Tom gazing through his bedroom window.

When bureau chief Bob Smith asked David and me to work on the Janet Jackson story, we jumped at the challenge of exposing a stalker in the act. I pictured us on the cover of *People* magazine, the first tabloid reporters in history to catch a stalker before the cops did. Our job sometimes mirrored that of private investigators. Any good reporter can get hold of home phone numbers, license plates, addresses, Social Security numbers, credit reports, restricted court documents, and so forth. The ease with which this is done is unnerving. If we can hunt them down, so can a stalker. We often had to disguise ourselves or take on false identities to get information from potential sources. Many people were apprehensive to speak with us at first, so we had to gain their trust by becoming part of the world they inhabited. Thanks to the media, celebrities don't have any privacy. We have sources at police stations, hospitals, and doctor's offices. If that isn't enough, housekeepers, personal trainers, airline operators, and even families are more than willing to sell us the dirt on their employees, clients, or next of kin.

To prepare for our Janet Jackson stakeout, David and I packed fifty dollars' worth of picnic supplies. We had decided to disguise ourselves as tourists who had wandered "accidentally" onto the *Poetic Justice* set. Getting on a film site is pretty easy because so many people are milling around the set. Our usual modus operandi would be to get past security by acting like we belong and then just blend in with everyone else, maybe even going as far as carrying equipment or taking part in a crowd scene.

But when we got to the set of *Poetic Justice,* it became immediately apparent that we wouldn't fit in: We were the only white people in sight. We promptly put our out-of-town, never-seen-a-film-set-before routine into action. We walked to the edge of the lawn where they were filming. As I unpacked our picnic lunch, David looked through his binoculars to try and zone in on Janet. He spotted her walking on the grass, flanked by two large black men with bulging muscles and permanent scowls. We proceeded to take notes surreptitiously and snap secret pictures with David's spy camera.

Suddenly we heard, "Hey, you guys! What the hell do you think you're doing?"

One of the stout guards was heading toward us, megaphone in one hand and walkie-talkie in the other. "What do you think you're doing?" repeated the guard. "Don't you see we're filming a movie here? Don't think I didn't see you with your little camera taking pictures. I ought to confiscate that thing and smash it against a tree."

"We're just visiting from Canada. On our honeymoon, actually," I said innocently. "We've never seen a movie being filmed before and thought it would be neat to take pictures to show the folks back home. But if that's not okay, we'll leave."

I began packing up our lunch as David tried to bargain with the guard. "How far away do we have to sit to qualify as not intruding on your shoot?" David asked.

"Listen, man, I could get you both thrown out of here right now, so why don't you take your things and get?"

"This is a public park," David insisted. "How could you get us thrown out of here?"

"Come on, honey, I think the man has made it clear that he wants us to leave," I uttered.

"But it's not fair. He doesn't own this park."

The guard stared at David with black eyes. We bolted.

Back at the car, David and I continued to keep an eye on the set and took turns sneaking behind a tree to get more photos. After three runs, we saw Stoutman charging at us like an enraged rhino. We immediately jumped into the car and peeled rubber. We decided to bag the entire assignment and retired to a Taco Bell for a ninety-nine-cent happy hour meal.

I've always thought how strange it must be to have bodyguards watch your every move. How menacing it would be to have crazed fans mail you their used underwear and send long letters professing their undying love for you along with a token of their affection—maybe a piece of their skin or a dead animal.

Some celebrities have been fortunate enough to catch their deranged fans. Michael J. Fox received nearly five thousand letters containing threats to his wife and child from a woman named Tina Ledbetter, who eventually ended up in jail. She was arrested five times. Another woman would break into David Letterman's house and cook him breakfast. Almost every celebrity, major and minor, has dealt with an obsessed fan at one time or another. Sometimes the fans are truck drivers, postal workers, or wanna-be actors; sometimes they're doctors, lawyers, and even cops.

Celebrities aren't the only ones who get harassed. There are times when the tables are turned and celebrities give reporters a taste of their own medicine. If a star finds out you've been digging too deep into his or her sordid past, the celeb will hire a private investigator to keep tabs on you. David has come home many times to find the back door of his house open and bubble gum wrappers scattered all over the kitchen floor; a true sign of private detectives having invaded your territory. He's also had his phone tapped, had notebooks stolen out of his car, and been followed by shady characters.

No matter how much they bitch and moan, some celebrities actually like the publicity they get from the rags. The more they're in the papers, the more their faces are seen, and the more famous they become. Having your photo plastered on the cover of the *Star* or the *National Enquirer* means you're a hot commodity. Agents and publicists have even tried to bolster a star's floundering career by calling us to sell dirt on their clients. They'll say things like, "So and so's career is a bit cold now. Can you print this truthful but scandalous story? It'll put them on the map again."

Of course, celebrities who are vehemently against a story we're about to print will go to enormous lengths to stop the presses. Even if they know the story is true, they'll threaten to sue, bomb the office, beat up the reporter, or engage in other unspeakable acts to stop us from airing their dirty laundry.

Naturally, we still air it. That's our job.

Trial by Fire
Los Angeles, California
July 1989

There was blood everywhere. Bits and pieces. Fragments of a girl named Rebecca scattered all over the lawn. It was a horrible sight, one that made the bile rise in my throat. But I had to be there. I had to cover this tragic, senseless murder. I was a reporter and had to take the detached role of investigating how such an event could have ever taken place. I had to ask the family questions, questions I knew they wouldn't want to answer, questions that would make me seem almost as cold and callous as the man capable of cold-blooded murder.

It was also one of my first assignments for the Star. *The victim: actress Rebecca Schaeffer, a promising twenty-one-year-old starlet who had warmed the hearts of the*

American public in her role opposite Pam Dawber on the television sitcom "My Sister Sam."

The killer: Robert John Bardo, a nineteen-year-old former janitor at a Jack-in-the-Box in Tucson, Arizona—an obsessed fan who took his twisted love for Rebecca to the ultimate extreme.

The crime: a horrible murder. Bardo rang Schaeffer's doorbell. When she answered, he pulled the trigger on a .357 Magnum, firing a single round that struck Rebecca in the chest.

I heard about the shooting on my police scanner on July 18, 1989, and quickly headed to Schaeffer's house. When I arrived, her body was still lying on the ground. Her head was twitching and her arms were moving slightly.

Police were everywhere, blocking hysterical neighbors from approaching the body. It was unbearable. I wanted to run like hell and get as far away as I could from this nauseating scene.

Reality set in.

I had to stay.

I spoke with one neighbor who had known Schaeffer for only a short while. "She was such a wonderful girl," said the woman. "So full of promise, so full of life. Why did this have to happen? What horrible animal could have done this to her?"

Then she broke down. An angry neighbor came over and scolded the woman for talking to me. "This guy is tabloid scum. Don't talk to him. All he's gonna do is make up lies about Rebecca."

I had tried to remain calm from the time I arrived, but it was becoming more difficult by the minute. I tried talking to the cops, but they were tight-lipped about the whole incident. They hadn't caught the murderer and were more concerned about that than getting their names in the paper.

Later that day, Bardo's sister called the police from Knoxville, Tennessee, and told them that her brother had telephoned her that morning, saying he was just blocks away from Schaeffer's residence. A local search was launched for Bardo, who was already on his way back to Tucson. He was caught by Tucson police while wandering on a highway in the downtown Tucson area, disoriented and trying to commit suicide by running toward oncoming cars. I wish one had hit him. Bardo was arrested and held in lieu of $1 million bail, then extradited to Los Angeles.

Later it was discovered that Bardo had started writing letters to Schaeffer two years earlier. On June 2, 1989, he had even appeared on the Warner Bros. lot where "My Sister Sam" was being filmed. He was carrying a teddy bear and roses and wanted to see Rebecca. A security guard wouldn't let him by. At the time, it was legal for citizens to obtain home addresses of celebrities by going to the Department of Motor Vehicles and paying five bucks for the honor. Bardo hired a private investigator in Los Angeles to get Schaeffer's address. The investigator called the DMV. Since her murder, the DMV has made that practice illegal, which makes the reporter's job a lot more difficult. To get addresses now, we have to run Social Security checks.

I contacted my police sources in Los Angeles, hoping for some new information. One of them told me that Bardo had allegedly gone to Schaeffer's residence twice on the day of the murder. They chatted for a few minutes. He told her what a big fan of hers he was and how much he admired her work. Then he left. After that, neighbors saw him wandering around the block a couple of times. They told police he looked kind of strange and disoriented, but they didn't think anything of it. An hour or so passed before Bardo went back to Schaeffer's house and fired the fatal shot.

Bardo later told police that he hadn't intended to kill Rebecca, but that he loved her so much he couldn't bear to see her with another man. If he couldn't have her, no one could.

I was used to dealing with sick cases, but none had affected me as deeply as this one. The Star told me to fly to

Portland, where Schaeffer grew up, and attend her funeral.
What a relaxing, cheerful event that would be. How could
I attend her funeral in the hopes of getting a good story out
of it? It seemed immoral and low.

I did it anyway.

The funeral was held on Sunday, July 23. Never before
in my life have I heard cries of anguish as I did that day.
They sounded more like animals howling than humans sobbing. Pam Dawber and her husband, Mark Harmon, joined
more than two hundred mourners as they paid tribute to
the fallen star.

I hovered near the outskirts of the crowd and felt dirty
and unwelcome. Even though no one knew who I was or
what I was there for, it felt wrong being there. I couldn't go
up to Rebecca's parents and ask how they felt. It was apparent how they felt; they had just lost a daughter. How
would any parent feel? My editors wanted me to ask
Schaeffer's boyfriend, Bradley Silberling, if Schaeffer had
been cheating on him with another man and how he felt
about that. It was a typical "line" for a story: Just as someone hits the lowest point, you find a way to kick the person
lower.

I left the funeral without doing my job. For once in my
life, I had to say fuck it, it wasn't worth it for me to get the
story. I didn't care. I just wanted to go home. I wanted to
leave this horrible nightmare, go back to my hotel room
and re-evaluate my life.

I had just started working for the tabloids and already
I'd had enough. Was this what it was going to be like? Invading people's privacy, witnessing sick events, and having
to compromise my sense of morality to get a story? I didn't
know if I could do it.

Cagney and Looney and Other Tales

Obsessed fans are the eeriest creatures we have to deal
with, aside from copy editors and our sources. I have

worked on a half dozen deranged-fan stories over the years, and after each one, I've always felt sullied in some way, as if I needed to run my brain through a mental car wash to rid myself of lingering traces of their madness.

The first and worst was Robert John Bardo, Rebecca Schaeffer's killer. Then there was Joanie Lee Penn, the kamikaze lesbian who broke into Sharon Gless's house armed with a .22-caliber assault-style rifle. She held the cops at bay for hours in Gless's bathroom. (Gless wasn't home.) Our take on the case was best expressed by the brilliant if twisted headline: CAGNEY AND LOONEY.

I once interviewed an extremely obsessed fan, Clarence Croutcher, who was fixated on Justine Bateman of "Family Ties." He lived in a depressing housing development near Rialto, California, with his sexually abused beagle, Tessie. Reporter Alvin Grimes and I found him stoned out of his mind on antidepressant medication, dialing his phone with his thumb, trying to reach the Tantric Love Center to optimize his penis for his new wife, Justine. On top of his TV were stacks of videotapes of "Family Ties" episodes and piles of rambling letters to Justine, pages long, with explicit illustrations in color crayon.

"How old is Tessie?" I asked Clarence.

"Tessie is forever," he said, casting an adoring gaze on the cringing mutt.

On his door were child's drawings and paintings of him done by the neighborhood urchins. I began to understand why celebs would flinch whenever fans surged toward them, screaming their name. You scan the faces in the crowd, not knowing which of them has some strange fantasy movie of you running in their head. They look just like everyone else. Maybe one of them has had a bad day and feels like making the front page with a photo of his gun and you lying in a heap on the sidewalk. Another Mark David Chapman or John Hinckley. As any writer knows, to do a coherent story, you have to understand it. You have to be able to look into the eyes of the people involved to be able to explain what the gist of the conflict is, to make the descriptions flow. Looking into the eyes of Clarence Croutcher left me with a dark, wrong feeling in the pit of my stomach, like I had swallowed a piece of putrefied roadkill.

Then Elfie Wade became obsessed with me. Elfie (her real name) had almost model-like looks—5'8", thin, blond, green eyes. She also had a habit of crawling around Sylvester Stallone's beach house, leaving letters in his mailbox, and peering into and scratching on his windows. The letters contained pieces of her flesh that she had hacked off, as well as rambling, threatening letters and pictures of John Lennon that had been stabbed again and again, with the word Imagine? scrawled across the top. Sly was only too happy to cooperate with us, because he figured the attention might spur the cops to take her seriously.

But before we can print an article that says a certain private citizen is a dangerous lunatic prone to disgusting antisocial behavior and should be locked up, we first have to check it out. Go and talk to her. Get her side of the story. Who knows? Maybe she's a jilted girlfriend with a legitimate complaint, and Stallone is just trying to use us to crush her and make her look bad. It was a dirty, dangerous job, and, of course, I was assigned to cover it.

Elfie lived in a modest house on a quiet, tree-lined street in a suburb of Los Angeles. The house looked too normal. Then again, what was I expecting—the Bates Motel? I walked up and knocked on the door. Elfie's housemate answered, a small, slight woman with a look of abject terror in her eyes.

"Can I speak to Elfie?" I asked.

In the background, I heard a woman scream, "Tell them to go away! Stop watching me! I mean it!"

The woman's eyes darted around, looking behind me, checking to see if I had any backup. I only wished. "Are you from the police? Are you coming to take her away?" I detected a note of hope in her voice.

"No, ma'am. I'm a reporter," I replied in my best Blues

Brothers imitation, handing her a Star magazine business card with my name on it. Her face whitened even more. She started closing the door. All the while, Elfie's screaming was climbing higher by the octave like an air-raid siren.

"Wait," I said. "Do you know what your roommate has been up to?"

"Yeah, the cops have been here several times and they've made it all very clear."

The door was still closing. Time to outrage her. "You're not in this thing together, are you?"

The door stopped. "What? Are you kidding! I've got nothing to do with this. I just sublet a room in my house. She's the one with the shrine, all the pictures and tapes, she's the one who follows Stallone everywhere, and . . ." She trailed off. Elfie had fallen silent and was obviously listening.

"If she's just boarding here, why don't you throw her out? If she's causing you so much trouble, wouldn't it be easier to evict her and not have to deal with it?"

Her control snapped. "You try living with a fucking lunatic and see how easy it is!"

Slam.

Photographer Alan Zanger and I staked out her place the rest of the week, hoping she'd leave and engage in stalking so we could get a shot of her in the act. No such luck. We just got a shot of her getting into and out of her economy car.

A couple of days later, I learned from Sly's bodyguards that Elfie had a .44 Magnum in the back of her car and fifty rounds of ammunition. I know something about ballistics. If Elfie had snapped and thrown down on us in the car during the stakeout, a .44 would have gone through the trunk, the rear seat, me, the front scat, the photographer, and the firewall, and split the engine block. The second shot would have done even more damage. I closed my eyes and shook my head.

A week later, the issue hit the stands. I was coming in from another assignment and walked into the office of Barry Levine, then the Los Angeles bureau chief. Barry was on the phone. An odd expression was on his face. Evidently Elfie was on the line. She was not pleased.

Barry hung up and darted to the front door, locking it. He gave me a sheepish look.

"Ah . . . that was Elfie. She's mad about the story, says it makes her look bad."

"No kidding. Well, did you tell her that stalking people sometimes makes you look bad?"

"Ah, well, she says she's going to get revenge. She followed Bev home, and Bev says somebody has been watching her walk her dogs all weekend. Now Elfie says she's going to come here and kill everybody."

"Everybody?"

"Well, especially you. She got the office address and your name off the card."

"Great. Just great."

"Now, don't get so upset, Dave. You know she'll probably never do anything. These people are all full of hot air."

"Yeah, right. Any other harmless assignments you'd like me to take on? Insulting John Gotti? Maybe you'd like me to go slash the tires on the lowriders of the Rolling 60's Crips?"

Elfie never did show up at the office. She eventually left Los Angeles and was arrested in the desert and institutionalized. But to this day, when I'm in the lowest level of a dark parking garage by myself and suddenly hear someone's footsteps behind me . . . I feel that little twinge.

4

DIRTY DEALS AND COMPROMISING POSITIONS

Trouble in Neverland
Santa Ynez, California
August 1993–February 1994

When pop star Michael Jackson was accused of molesting a thirteen-year-old boy, most of the country thought the allegations were ludicrous. How could such a famous figure, who gave tons of his time and money to children's charities, molest little boys? It wasn't possible.

Or was it?

David and I received a frantic call from Bob Smith early one Saturday morning ordering us to head out immediately to Michael Jackson's Neverland Ranch in Santa Ynez, California, about a three-hour drive from Los Angeles.

"I want you both to get there in two hours and I don't care if you get a speeding ticket. Just move your ass," were his exact words.

"What's going on?" I asked.

"Jackson has fucking molested a young boy. It hasn't

even hit the papers yet, so get going because I want you both to be the first ones on the scene before it turns into a zoo up there."

Due to traffic, we got to the ranch in a little over four hours and went to work on what would become one of the biggest news stories in tabloid history.

Michael's Encino mansion, as well as his home at Neverland Ranch and his Century City condominium, had already been searched by police. To break into the many secret rooms Michael keeps in all of his residences, the police had to hire locksmiths. A pal of mine, who works at the condo where Michael resided, told me he had seen the inside of the place when he let the police in. He said the inside looked like Disneyland, filled with enormous stuffed animals, toys, trains, electronic games, and a life-size statue of Mickey Mouse.

"It was eerie," said my source. "It was like the home of a five-year-old kid, not a grown man. I mean, I've heard of keeping yourself young at heart, but this is ridiculous."

He also told me he wasn't ever allowed to look inside the locked secret rooms. He heard they contained even wilder statues, odd games, and toys. The police left with numerous boxes of items, but the source got only a glimpse of a stack of videotapes, a photo album, and a few cassette tapes.

All we knew so far was that the accuser was a thirteen-year-old former close friend of Jackson's and that he and Jackson had traveled around the world together. We didn't know the boy's name, his home address, or what the specific details of the charges were. David knew from his various police contacts that it was impossible to obtain a search warrant without extensive probable cause, especially with a superstar like Jackson. The cops didn't want to chance messing up a high-profile case like this, so before they even informed the media about their actions, they looked into the validity of the charges with great scrutiny.

Until this incident, most people regarded Michael as one of the kindest, most generous people on earth. Although he was perceived as being strange because of his obsession with plastic surgery, his love of toy stores, and his childlike qualities, most people shrugged these off as being a unique part of the pop star. "He's just a kid at heart, a superstar who never experienced a childhood of his own," was a common statement among Jackson fans.

When David and I arrived in Santa Ynez, the story hadn't exploded yet. News teams and local reporters were just starting to learn about the situation, but the public hadn't been informed yet about the allegations.

The silence didn't last for long.

By six o'clock that night, it was all over the news. We knew that the small town of Santa Ynez, with its one post office, two general stores, and local diner, would be swarming with reporters by the next morning. We had to get cracking on the story.

We went to the diner to see if we could get information from any of the locals. Over ham-and-cheese sandwiches and Diet Cokes, we heard two men talking about the police search at Jackson's ranch. We didn't want to disrupt their conversation by blatantly asking if they knew anything about the Jackson case, so we took turns walking nonchalantly past them in order to home in on their conversation.

"I couldn't believe they just barged in there and took over the place," said one of the guys.

"And hiring a locksmith to open the joint. That was real smooth," added the other. "I bet this is going to get real messy."

"So do you think he did it?"

"I don't know. It makes me sick to think about it, but you've got to admit, he is kind of strange."

"You can say that again."

"At first, I thought his having an amusement park was just for the kids. You know, a gesture of love toward children in need. But when I saw him night after night playing by himself on the merry-go-round, I started to think something was up. What grown man spends his evenings on a merry-go-round? By himself? But molesting a kid. I don't know if Michael is capable of doing it. I've never seen him get too close to the young boys, if you know what I mean."

"What if they find some evidence, like kiddie porn tapes or photos?"

"You're making me sick with this talk. Let's go."

When the men got up to leave, I followed them out while David got their license plate numbers. I ran up to one of them and asked if I could have a moment of his time. He said sure and told me he and his pal worked at the Neverland Ranch as gardeners.

"I don't know much more about the case than has already been said," he told me. "But if you want to get some really juicy dirt on the case, call this guy." He wrote down the name of another gardener who had been fired from the Jackson ranch only a few days earlier because he supposedly "knew too much."

I left my number and informed the man that he would be adequately compensated if he ever learned any further details and divulged them to me. Many sources loosen up with time—and money. People who won't talk at the first meeting often spill their guts when the rent comes due.

David and I went by Jackson's ranch every few hours to keep tabs on the situation. Because Michael was out of the country on a concert tour, nothing much was going on. The police couldn't release the identity of the boy due to his age, so we were left to dig up the information on our own.

That night, back at our hotel, a pal of David's called and said he had photos of Michael and the young boy. We knew the alleged molestation took place when Michael and the boy were on a trip to Las Vegas, and luckily this pal happened to be in Las Vegas at the same time and got a few shots of them together. David called his source at the police department and got a description of the boy, but only after he promised the cop some big bucks. Then he asked his friend to describe the boy in the photo.

Both descriptions matched.

David was elated. He started dancing and singing around the room, thinking his pal was the only one who had photos and that his buddy could make huge amounts of money selling the shots around the world. He was talking $100,000 or more. I told him to calm down, because I knew it was crazy to jump the gun. But David felt sure the cash would come, so I backed off. Needless to say, the money never came. Once the papers found out they couldn't show the boy's face in print due to his age, the value of any photos went down immensely.

Details about the alleged molestation came out in the papers a few days later. The British tabloids, American tabloids, all the news programs, and the legitimate papers each had their own version of what they thought took place between Jackson and the kid. An American reporter was able to get hold of the intake case, which contained what the boy told a social worker the night he reported being molested. It revealed graphic, sexual details describing what Michael allegedly did to the boy and what the boy did to Michael in return. The acts included oral sex, mutual fondling, sleeping together in the same bed, and taking baths together. These accusations weren't light; they were explicit, damaging, and profound enough to put Michael behind bars for a very long time.

The immediate reaction from the Jackson camp was that the accusations were a failed extortion attempt on the part of the young boy's father, who had showbiz aspirations. Supposedly the father wanted to land a $20 million production deal from Jackson to finance his own films. When the extortion attempt went sour, the father allegedly instructed his son to accuse Michael of molesting him. The father, a prominent Beverly Hills dentist with a large celebrity clientele, wasn't hard up for money at all. Before the accusations surfaced, he had sold a story idea to Hollywood that resulted in the Mel Brooks spoof *Robin Hood: Men in Tights*.

The boy's mother, divorced from the dentist and remarried to the owner of a popular car rental business, told the press she was shocked by the allegations and had no idea these activities had been going on between Jackson and her son.

Over the next few days, I spoke to many Santa Ynez locals who gave us their forthright opinions about the case. One woman, a former employee of Jackson's who did not want to be identified, said, "I've personally never seen Michael do anything out of the ordinary when he was around children, but that doesn't mean nothing took place. I have a teenage son and I know he wouldn't accuse someone of molesting him if it wasn't true. Taking on one of the world's biggest entertainers isn't something you do for money. There would be too much for the boy to lose and for Michael to gain if the boy was totally lying. I've got to believe there's at least one grain of truth in the child's story. But that's just my opinion."

Another local raised the question, "If Michael loves children so much, then why is he always hanging out with young boys and not young girls? Why don't girls travel with him, go on shopping sprees, and hang out at his ranch?"

David had the brilliant idea of trying to sneak onto the Jackson ranch. Mind you, the ranch is secured by barbed-wire fences, infrared devices, cameras, and security guard posts, so breaking in wouldn't be the easiest or the wisest decision in the world. But David was persistent. He wanted to get close-up photos of the ranch and, at the same time, spy on the goings-on using his extremely powerful binoculars. We drove down a private dirt road that led to the back entrance of the ranch. We were almost to the entrance when a cop spotted us, flashed on his lights, and told us point-blank, "Get the hell out of the area or you'll be arrested!" We got out.

Over the next few weeks, many former employees of Jackson's began speaking out about everything from having witnessed Jackson molesting young boys to having kept diaries about his actions for their own use. The tabloid television shows began a feeding frenzy, offering ludicrous amounts of money to any former employee who was willing to spill the beans.

I wanted to find out more about exactly what would be needed to prosecute someone of Michael Jackson's stature. Just when talk of Jackson offering the boy a $20 million settlement began, David and I attended a lecture in Brentwood, California, where Lauren Weis, acting head deputy district attorney in charge of sex crimes and child abuse in Los Angeles County, who was also heading the Michael Jackson investigation, spoke about legal issues and famous court cases.

We attended the lecture under the pretense that we were fashion photographers who happened to be deeply interested in the justice system. David had heard horror stories about Lauren Weis saying that she was one of the harshest prosecutors in the county—a woman whom you wouldn't want to face in court. I was surprised when I came face-to-face with this so-called tough chick, who stood a mere 5'3", with sandy blond hair, porcelain skin, and a huge Pepsodent smile. She spoke first about the Erik and Lyle Menendez murder trial, then the John Wayne Bobbitt trial, and finally about the Michael Jackson case. She made it clear that she couldn't talk extensively about the Jackson case because the investigation was still in progress.

"How do they prove a man's guilt in a regular case, not one involving someone as big as Michael Jackson?" I inquired.

"In most cases, all they need is a child's testimony in order to press charges against the man or woman being accused of child molestation," explained Weis. "The most difficult thing is to prove a defendant's guilt when there isn't any physical evidence. Maybe he touched a child or had the child touch him, but that doesn't leave any scars. A child saying "He did it" is what the court uses to prosecute. The older the child is, the more weight they put on his testimony. A younger kid is more impressionable and is often swayed by the advice of adults. Many young children have been talked into believing that someone did something to them, when in fact nothing happened at all."

I pressed for more details. "In the case of Michael Jackson, how much more do they need in order to issue a warrant for his arrest?"

Another prosecutor on the case answered, "They're going to need physical evidence in the form of videotapes, photos, or scars on the child. Or, the child himself will have to testify against Jackson in order to make the case stand."

"Can they force a child to testify?" I asked.

"No," said Weis. "You can't force any victim of a sexual crime to testify against the perpetrator. That's why it'll be hard to build a case against Jackson if the kid doesn't want to take the stand."

After the lecture, David followed Lauren out into the parking lot and asked her about the status of the case. She was bitter and confirmed what she had only dropped hints about: that the case was going to fizzle out because the child wouldn't testify.

"Did Jackson's money have anything to do with that?" David asked.

"Jackson's money has been a factor in this case since the word go," Weis responded wearily. "Every time we think we've got someone or some evidence, somehow it all disappears."

In January 1994, a resolution in the civil suit case between Jackson and the boy was reached, and all Jackson had to do was dish out a mere $29 million to keep the boy's mouth shut. The criminal investigation continued but was eventually dropped at the end of 1994. No criminal charges were ever filed.

Although Michael's lawyers insisted that the settlement was in no way an admission of guilt on Michael's part, the question on many people's minds was: If Jackson was innocent, why would he pay off the kid?

To shut him up?

To avoid going to court?

To put the entire ordeal behind him?

We may never know.

Michael dropped a bombshell of his own when he married "the King's" daughter, Lisa Marie Presley, in a private ceremony in the Dominican Republic in May of 1994. Lisa Marie, who only months earlier had divorced Danny Keough, a down-to-earth musician from Nebraska with whom she had two kids, was rumored to be using Jackson to get her own singing career off the ground.

And I thought Julia Roberts marrying Lyle Lovett after only two weeks of courtship was strange. Hollywood was becoming a regular circus when it came to walking down the aisle. Marriages in Tinseltown were a dime a dozen. This is not to say many of these marriages lasted. Celebrities kept their leased Mercedes longer than they kept their spouses.

Everyone speculated that Michael and Lisa's marriage was a business deal. It was a common rumor in Hollywood that stars often married in order to keep their sexual preferences a secret or to bolster their career or their image as a family man or woman. After the molestation charges, Michael's image was severely tarnished. He needed positive publicity, and fast. Enter Lisa Marie. Elvis's once hard-edged, spoiled little daughter was now a doting mom, a faithful member of the Church of Scientology, and a drug-free role model. The perfect package to save Jackson's faltering image.

Still, some people swore the couple were madly in love and married only to strengthen their ties of devotion. But other insiders said that even if they did marry for love, Michael's troubles were far from over. In February 1995, divorce papers were filed by the father of the boy Michael was accused of molesting. The father stated that his marriage to the boy's stepmother had crumbled under the stress of the civil suit and that he was now broke. The papers also revealed that not only had Michael paid the boy a pretty penny, but he had also agreed to pay the father and the boy's stepmother a lump sum of a million dollars apiece!

The final blow came in 1996, when Michael and Lisa Marie divorced. End of story? Hardly. With an enigmatic superstar like Michael, you never know what might happen next.

Family Sellouts
Monterey, California
September 1991

The best advice I can give to any young celebrity who is trying to figure out how to deal with his or her newfound fame is: Take care of your family. After all, they know where your skeletons are located. If a family member decides to sell you down the river, be prepared for a veritable white-water rafting trip.

Mind you, your family will do it. The combination of money and a chance to avenge a petty slight proves to be too much of a temptation. For Nick Savalas, the idea of wreaking revenge on his hated sister, actress Nicolette Sheridan of TV's "Knots Landing," was more alluring than the money itself, although the Star *paid him $25,000 for his trouble.*

Nicolette is widely regarded as the most venomous, backbiting, unpleasant bitch in town. In 1990, after she and actor Harry Hamlin of "L.A. Law" were engaged, I called her publicist to get a "reaction" to the story.

"What has that bitch done now?" he spat.

I almost dropped the phone. I thought he was joking. "Uh, I was just calling to see if you had a reaction to Harry Hamlin leaving his wife for Nicolette?"

"He's doing that?"

"Yeah, they say they're going to get married."

"Oh, great. Well, I've got this to say: They deserve each other. And you can print that." Slam.

When the people you pay to say nice things about you start referring to you as a bitch, it's probably time to take a long, hard look at your interpersonal relationships.

But a year later there I was in Monterey, California, covering the Sheridan-Hamlin merger. The blessed event took place at a remote ranch in a narrow canyon. The guests paraded around in 1920s costumes in a large, dress-up croquet party. I looked down from atop a hill half a mile across the valley, steadying a huge zoom lens as Alan Zanger took pictures of the indistinct shapes.

Nicolette didn't know it yet, but her marriage was already in trouble. Nick Savalas had been at Harry Hamlin's bachelor party earlier that week and had sold us some of the most incriminating photos I had ever seen. They showed Harry sitting in his underwear, a dazed but gleeful expression on his face, as one stripper stuck her head between his thighs and another maneuvered his head toward her crotch. When the shot ran on the cover of the Star, *all the explicit organs were covered with black strips, but on Harry's shoulder was a large, dripping wad of semen. I still can't believe the* Star *got away with that.*

Nick was in the wedding party and was supposed to take pictures but we thought he might flake out on us, so we proceeded as though we were going to get nothing from him. Julian buzzed the ranch again and again in a small, light helicopter, his low-level passes spooking the horses at the ranch into running into the paddock fences and one another.

"The ranch owner went haywire," Julian later recounted. "He drove out to the airfield, found us on the tarmac, walked up, kicked my pilot right in the balls, and started screaming that he was going to shoot all of us." Barrage balloons went up to try to keep the choppers from flying too low.

As the day wore on, Barry became more and more

desperate to get someone with a camera onto the premises. Finally, Barry, Donna, Peter, and I hiked to a gated housing development near the wedding site. The development was closed. We waited. The gate opened, a car came out, and we scooted in. We walked up and down steep hills, crossed barbed-wire fences, and finally came to a wide, deep stream. On the other side was a road leading right to the wedding. All along the way, I had noticed a lot of poison oak, and on the other side of the water was a thick forest of the noxious weed. We also saw security guards patrol the road every few minutes. Crossing the stream to get to the road had as much potential for success as a headlong charge into a solid brick wall.

Barry started stripping off his shoes and socks and rolling up his pants. "Barry, that's suicide." I warned. "You're gonna wind up in jail."

I don't know what was driving him, but that day he went beyond what most people would consider reasonable or even sane. He and Donna waded in and promptly slipped in the mud. They were forced to dog-paddle their way across. Barry lost his camera and listening device in the first slide, and his wallet in another one.

"Watch out for the red stuff. That's poison oak," I called out. Later, Barry told me they had climbed all the way up a steep hill to within twenty yards of the wedding tents, only to be immediately caught by security before they could hear or see anything. The guards cursed them and hurled rocks down the slope after them. And if that wasn't bad enough, Barry developed a full-body case of poison oak and didn't come into the office for a week. But at 9 A.M. the morning after the wedding, Barry, nervous as I've ever seen him, told me to drive by the ranch to "pick someone up." The "someone" turned out to be Nick Savalas. He was obviously trying very hard to look like James Dean: He had the white T-shirt, black leather jacket, and jeans down pat, and he was chain-smoking. But Dean's ineffable cool seemed to

elude him. Nick had a story and a roll of film with him and was nervous to the point of panic. I drove him to a restaurant. Barry soon joined us, scratching himself as we sat down to negotiate. The price for the film and story was $25,000. The problem was Star's New York office didn't know if it was worth that without seeing it. So we had to get the film developed, which made Nick even more nervous.

"Nicolette is such a bitch," he kept saying. "I hope this fuckin' makes her cry all night. She's just a stuck-up little cunt. She's not going to find out who sold this, is she?"

"Naah, there were lots of people in there with cameras," I assured him. "When the pics appear, just act cool for the next couple of weeks. They'll never be able to figure out where they came from."

Subsequently, Nick took the $25,000, bought a new Harley, and took his girlfriend, actress Milla Jovovich, to Las Vegas on a lavish all-expense-paid trip. And he wonders how they figured out the photos came from him.

But the last double-cross was reserved for us at the Star. Despite the long hours we had put in coddling Nick, despite the money we spent on the pictures and covering the wedding, despite all-out effort, poison oak, and swollen testicles, we didn't wind up with an exclusive. Why? Dick Kaplan, the Star editor, responding to complaints from the Enquirer that they had gotten scooped twice in a row on a big story (look to your lazy reporters would be my advice), decided to GIVE the photos and exclusive story to the Enquirer so they wouldn't LOOK like such idiots. What did we get in return? Screwed.

Mr. Murdoch on Line Three

In the summer of 1989, when the Star was still owned by Rupert Murdoch and his multimedia empire was tottering, an Enquirer reporter came into our office with notes for a blockbuster story he had computer-hacked out of the Enquirer's system around the time he was acrimoniously *fired. It was about Demi Moore's mother, and it was nasty. The* Enquirer *had hushed up the story in return for exclusive interviews with Bruce Willis and Demi. The* Star *wanted me to take the information and rain on their parade. I ran down the list of names and numbers, and a sick, twisted portrait began to emerge.*

Since then, Virginia Guynes-Moore has become a regular media whore, falling down the ladder of respectability as her drug addictions drove her to sell stories to everyone. In the end, she was too slimy for even the Globe *to tolerate.*

But at the time, the revelations I was hearing were new. Turncoat drug buddies she owed money to offered to sell me photos of her smoking crack, snorting coke, giving blow–jobs to dealers in exchange for drugs, and so forth. Sources said her first husband, Demi's father, had died mysteriously in a garage-car exhaust incident ruled as a suicide. They hinted darkly that Virginia had done him in for the insurance money, and they offered to sell bank records that showed how she had drained the account of Demi's brother, Morgan, taking all his inheritance money. I saw records of her four failed marriages and evidence that Virginia had committed bigamy by marrying two, maybe three guys at the same time. I read police reports about how she was hog-tied and gagged after she bit a New Mexico cop after one of her many DUI arrests. I kept calling and writing and hounding Virginia until she finally cracked and was ready to talk for money. And then it happened again. The double cross, another dirty deal.

Murdoch's studio, 20th Century-Fox, had not had a hit movie in more than a year. They were in negotiations with Bruce Willis to get him to star in Die Hard 2. *Bruce wanted the truth about Virginia suppressed. He called Murdoch and said something akin to "Get this reporter off my case or I'm not doing the movie."*

Result: "Mr. Murdoch on line three for you, Dave."

I was told we could still do a story, but it was going to be a "nice" story. I was told to write the story so that readers would squeeze out tears of pity for Demi and her poor mom. I was told to lie like hell and make this woman sound like an upstanding citizen and loving mother who cared for her daughter.

I did it.

5

PRAISE THE LORD AND PASS THE VIDEO CAMERA: CELEBRITY WEDDINGS

Tommy Lee and Tabloid Footsie
Cancun, Mexico
January 1995

*E*very tabloid wants a wedding on its cover; it sells. *Celebrity weddings make the homemakers of America go all squishy inside and dream their dreams of what should have been—a lovely ceremony in some exotic tropical hideaway, a big, tall, handsome groom beside them—rather than what was—a Justice of the Peace, a Twinkie wedding cake, and a honeymoon in a trailer park.*

The wedding of "Baywatch" beauty Pamela Anderson to rocker Tommy Lee was made to order for the tabloids, and I had the dubious honor of being the first to know about it. One bright Sunday afternoon, I received a phone call from Bob Smith to go to an address in the San Fernando Valley and interview a woman named Bobbie Brown. She had phoned the office and said she had a huge story about a secret wedding but wouldn't reveal anything until she received a contract for a bundle of cash.

"The *Bobbie Brown?*" I asked. "The one who was recently beaten up by Tommy Lee in Malibu? The blonde in all the Warrant videos?"

"I dunno. Just getcher ass over there," Bob said.

I arrived at the address to find it was indeed the *Bobbie Brown,* red-eyed and still visibly upset, sitting and drinking with her friends, complaining about what a rat Tommy was.

We quickly began playing "tabloid footsie." The banter unfolds like so: "What have you got?" "How much is it worth to you?" "I can't tell you until I know what it is." "I won't tell you until I know how much you'll pay."

Finally we arrived at the tentative figure of $25,000 for the exclusive story.

"Tommy's in Cancun marrying Pam Anderson. And it's going down right this second," Bobbie blurted out as she gulped down a glass of wine. The details quickly spilled forth. Bobbie herself had been engaged to Tommy until a week ago, when he flew into a rage, screamed in her face, smashed two telephones against the wall, and threw a wine bottle at her head.

Bobbie said her relationship with Tommy had been on the rocks for the past couple of months. She added that she was out of money since Tommy wouldn't allow her to continue her modeling career, and she needed cash bad or else she wouldn't be doing this. She wove a story of childish jealousy and revenge, bitterness, strange sex, and faithlessness.

This story would positively leap off the stands. If we were the only ones who knew about a wedding this big, we could get photos of them while they were still in Cancun. The pictures would be worth a fortune, as would the story. I interviewed Bobbie for hours, and she poured out all the pain she was feeling. In the middle of our conversation, her mother called, and she had a rip-roaring fight with her over the phone about Tommy.

In only a few short hours, though, everything began to unravel. Someone leaked the story, and news of the wedding spread like wildfire. Bob Smith and Dick Belsky, the news editor, called me up to say that since the story was no longer exclusive, Star wouldn't pay $25,000 for it. They would now only pay $5,000. And I was the one who had to call Bobbie and break the bad news to her.

Then Bob told me I was booked on the 1:30 A.M. flight to Cancun. By the time I arrived in the resort town, exhaustion permeated my entire being. I wanted to bag the whole assignment and veg out on the beach, but I couldn't. I was supposed to check into the posh Camino Real Hotel with super-hyper photographer Alan Zanger and track down fellow hotel guests Tommy and Pamela.

The story I'd heard was that Pamela had originally gone down to Cancun with her boyfriend, surfer Kelly Slater. Tommy was also there and had more than just a passing interest in the busty blonde. Pamela and Kelly had even switched hotels a couple of times to get away from Tommy. She had no interest in the wild rocker and wanted to enjoy a peaceful vacation. Tommy tracked her down and persuaded her to go out with him. When she finally gave in, he fed her the drug Ecstasy and booze and convinced her he was the perfect man for her. She immediately dumped Slater and spent the next four days living it up with Tommy in Mexico.

On their fifth day of dating, Tommy got down on one knee and proposed. And of course, the only logical thing for a strait-laced, rational woman like Pam to do was to say yes. After all, isn't four days more than enough time to get to know someone and make a decision to spend the rest of your life with that person?

After checking into our rooms, Zanger and I walked through the lobby and onto the beach, where we looked to see if Pam and Tommy were out sunning themselves. I tried *calling Pam's room, but the line was busy. I figured the phone was off the hook.*

I left to make a call to the editors at the Star *to tell them where we were and what we were doing. I got back to find Zanger frozen in his chair. Pam had just walked by on her way to the elevators from the hotel restaurant. Tommy and his buddy followed a couple of minutes later. We were able to ID them only by the tattoos they had running down their arms.*

Minutes later, we spotted them checking out of the hotel. They had a cart piled high with luggage. This was it. They were leaving, and this would be our only chance to get pictures.

I leaned against a wall and Zanger crouched down, stuck a long lens under my armpit, and started shooting. He got an entire roll of them kissing, hugging, and cuddling. I could feel his hands tremble with excitement and see beads of sweat rolling down his face.

A curious woman walked up. "What's all the commotion here?" she asked.

I said, "Nothing. We were just taking some pictures of the hotel lobby. We're interested in architecture."

But she walked around the corner, saw Pam and Tommy, and decided to be a good Samaritan. "Hey, those guys were taking your picture," she called out, pointing to us. Pam immediately summoned hotel security, who told us to leave the premises.

Zanger wanted to stay to try to shoot some video, but I said, "Enough's enough. Don't get greedy, or we'll get busted, they'll take the film, and we'll wind up with nothing."

He agreed and I dragged him toward a side exit I had spotted earlier. Unfortunately, we wound up directly behind Tommy as he went from store to store, buying Pam all kinds of little presents. Suddenly he turned around and recognized us.

Uh-oh.

I'd been told Tommy was a real nut when it came to the

press, and that he would charge at you without warning. We bolted past him and out into the parking lot. We knew what flight Tommy and Pam were taking out of Cancun, so we went to the airport and waited by the check-in counter. When they arrived, Zanger shot even more photos of the couple smooching up a storm. He got video of Tommy and Pam trying to explain why they had so much luggage and sweating at the thought of customs agents asking them to open it. Then two of Tommy's buddies spotted us and came charging over, red-faced with anger. "Hey! Stop taking pictures! We saw you following Tommy all over the place. Get out of here!" they yelled.

The other tourists gave us puzzled looks. Zanger ducked his head and mumbled an apology. The minute their backs were turned, he started shooting again.

Finally Pam and Tommy went to their plane. Alan was so buzzed with excitement he couldn't stand still. He was heading back on the next plane with his film and video, since he didn't trust the airlines to deliver it. He couldn't wait to get on the horn and start syndicating. I, however, felt like a boxer in a late round, punished, exhausted, bleary, and swaying on my feet. I was going to stay in Cancun to try to pick up more details about what they had been doing while in town, then file the story by phone.

I drove back to the hotel zone and started nosing around at the gift shops and bars, using my Spanish to get the kind of details magazines love to use to flesh out stories. I learned Tommy had followed Pamela around town from hotel to hotel until he was able to get her to go out with him. Then, after a night of doing shots of tequila, he started licking her face. It was like a police recreation of a crime. I had to try to dog their footsteps and get a picture of what their life was like in the last two weeks.

I went back to the hotel, lay down for just a second, and woke up eight hours later to hear the phone ringing. My editors wanted a status report. I was initially cocky and triumphant, telling them that not only had we found Tommy and Pam, but that we had gotten pictures of them as well. That's when they broke the bad news to me. While I had been comatose, a couple of Brit reporters had come to Cancun, gotten their hands on some film, and were now flogging it all over the world. The pics Alan had taken turned out to be too dark and indistinct to use, so they wanted me to find out whether any of the tourists had taken pictures of the wedding ceremony on the beach.

I walked over to the beach and immediately ran into a group of giggling young college girls from Michigan who said they had been there and seen the whole thing. Trying to remain calm, I walked them over to the bar, bought them all a round of drinks, and asked if they happened to take any pictures.

"Sure did! Got the whole thing, even the part where Tommy threw Pam in the water and her top came off!" one girl squealed.

I almost fell off my bar stool with shock and elation. A dream come true! Then her next sentence hit me like a bucket of ice water.

"We sold the film to this English guy for a hundred bucks," the girl chortled. "Boy did we take him to the cleaners. It's paying for the rest of our vacation here."

I slumped forward in agony and defeat, resting my head against the cool, boozy wood of the bar. I began to pound my skull against my coaster. The bartender gave me a frightened look and shrank back, muttering, "Loco Gringo."

"What's wrong? What's wrong?" the girl said, alarmed. "He said he'd be back by noon, so we can sell the pictures to you then."

"Gyaah," I moaned. "It doesn't matter. Those pictures were worth at least twenty-five thousand. And those guys who paid you a hundred? They're selling them around the world right now for hundreds of thousands. Mas tequila, por favor." The bartender leaped into action.

"But the guy promised he'd give us the negatives once

he got the film developed," cried one of the other girls. "He said he was just making copies and would meet us here later."

"Say good-bye to your film," I told them, "because he won't be back."

Later I wandered around in a haze, picking up more details. I spoke to a source at the hotel who told me, "Pamela wore a skimpy white bikini as her wedding 'gown' and Tommy wore a pair of black shorts. After they said their 'I dos,' Tommy picked up Pam and threw her into the water. When she stood up, her bikini top fell off, much to the delight of every guy on the beach. Then they began kissing and didn't stop for over five straight minutes. They didn't seem to care that everyone on the beach was staring. They were in a world of their own."

The couple spent a short honeymoon in a $1,500-a-night suite at the Camino Real. When they got back to L.A., they celebrated with friends at the ultratrendy restaurant/bar Sanctuary, which Anderson co-owns. It was back in L.A. that Pamela started getting warnings from friends of Tommy's two ex-lovers. A copy of the police report that contained information on Tommy's arrest for allegedly abusing and battering Bobbie Brown was faxed to Pam's office. Friends say Tommy hit the two women and pushed them around on more than one occasion.

"Tommy gets nasty when he's jealous," said a pal of Bobbie's. "He'll fly off the handle for no reason at all and then turn things around to make you look like the bad guy. He pushed Bobbie around just because an old boyfriend phoned her to see how she was doing. He's totally irrational and possessive, and if Pamela thinks she knows him after only four days, she's going to be in for a rude awakening."

So far, however, the happy couple have rarely been off the front pages of the tabloids, whether it's nude photos, porn tapes, screaming fights, near-breakups, pregnancies, tattoos. They're the new Tom and Roseanne, celebs locked in a crazy marriage that America can't seem to get enough of.

Leading Lady Hooks Lyle and His Large Band
Indianapolis, Indiana
June 1994

All I wanted was to get some sleep. Just a few hours. I had been working around the clock, and I was beyond exhausted; I was mentally depleted of life. My body ached for a nice, warm bed with down pillows and a big, soft comforter. At 11:30 in the evening, I finally got my wish. Just as I began to doze off into my magical dream world, the phone rang.

David answered it and then tried to wake me, but to no avail. "Honey, Tony Frost from the *Enquirer* is on the phone. He wants you to go out of town right now!" he shouted.

I didn't stir.

After three minutes of repeated wake-up attempts, I finally came to life and hobbled to the phone. Since I had never been sent on an out-of-town assignment by the *Enquirer,* the call caught me by surprise.

"Hi," I said. "What's going on?"

Tony started to speak in his usual low, sneaky voice. "Lysa, I've got an out-of-town assignment for you. But before I tell you any information, I need to know if I can trust you not to tell David about it. I need your word that you won't reveal the information I disclose to you until the assignment is over."

"You have my word," I said.

"You'll be working on one of the biggest breaking stories of the year," he continued. "I'll need you to catch a plane in one hour. Can you do that?"

I glanced at the clock. It read 11:45 P.M.

"Can I trust you?" Tony asked again. "This is a top

secret assignment, and I need to know that I can trust you. Can I?"

I felt like I was talking to a broken record.

"Yes, Tony, my little paranoid friend, you can trust me." I assured him that I would not tell David, and that yes, I could leave town in one hour.

That wasn't enough for him. He had to get my unwavering promise, an eternal oath. Rolling my eyes, I swore to him that I would keep my mouth shut and that he could have my firstborn child if I broke my promise. But that still wasn't enough. He told me he'd call back in five minutes. In the meantime, I was supposed to pack my things and get ready to leave.

I raced around the house like a junkie in need of a hit, frantically throwing mismatched clothing into my suitcase. I was awake, wired, and ready to go.

Tony called back exactly five minutes later. "I'm sorry to have woken you," he uttered. "The story is off. We don't need you to go out of town after all. But you will get paid for the inconvenience of being woken up."

At this point, I was convinced that Tony was a pathological liar. I knew the story wasn't off and he was just afraid I'd leak the information to the *Star*. He kept saying how sorry he was to have bothered me and how I'd get paid adequately for my time. I inhaled the bull, said goodnight, and hung up the phone. I didn't care about going out of town. I just wanted to go back to bed.

Such is the tabloid business. The phone rang again a minute later, and guess who it was? Tony. He said he was sorry to bother me, but that miraculously, the story was on once again. After I promised and swore a zillion more times that I wouldn't leak the story, he finally coughed up the details.

Julia Roberts and Lyle Lovett were getting married.

Yeah, right, I thought, *and Cindy Crawford is pregnant with President Clinton's baby.* If the story was actually true, I would be stunned, flabbergasted, and utterly confused about the mental state of the human race. I couldn't believe that America's Pretty Woman was going to marry Lyle, the country crooner, a man she'd only known for two weeks.

I knew of Lyle because of his small role in Robert Altman's brilliant film *The Player*. I didn't know he was a cowpunk singer; I didn't even know what cow-punk was. But nevertheless, I was a risk-taker, a thrill-seeker, a tabloid reporter, and I told Tony I'd go to Indianapolis and check things out.

I got off the phone and immediately told David everything.

I knew he wasn't going to leak the information to the *Star* because our relationship wasn't like that. Although I'm sure many tabloid reporters wouldn't think twice about selling out their spouses, David and I would never betray each other's trust. David freaked when he heard the story and thought it was bogus. "At least I'll get a free trip to Indiana," I told him. "A nice hotel, some good meals, rest and relaxation. It could be worse. I could be going to Death Valley."

I looked at the clock. It was now 12:40 A.M. My plane was due to take off at 1:30 and I had to haul ass. I threw some more clothes into the suitcase and took off. We got to the airport in fifteen minutes, a trip that usually takes thirty, and I made the plane with one minute to spare. I slept about two hours during the flight and ate nothing—a feat I would regret over the next twenty-four hours, when food wasn't an option and neither was sleep.

From the moment I landed in Indianapolis, I found myself on a wild-goose chase that lasted three days. I met up with paparazzo Larry Kaplan at the airport, and we began our search for Julia and Lyle. Tony had no idea where the couple was getting married or what hotel they were staying in. All he knew was that they were somewhere in Indianapolis. Larry suggested we check out the Omni Hotel downtown. He'd heard from a buddy that the wedding party might be staying there.

As luck would have it, when we arrived I saw tour buses loading up guests dressed in formal attire. I quickly called Larry Haley, the editor in charge of the story, and reported what I had seen. He told me to look out for Lyle and not to go anywhere until I spotted him. While I was on the phone, Lyle walked right by me. Fate was definitely on my side. I've had this sort of thing happen to me before, but this time I was stunned to see Lyle because I still thought the entire story was a hoax.

Lyle got on the bus, and it started to pull away. I quickly located Kaplan, who was changing into his suit in the men's room, and we ran to our separate cars to follow the caravan of buses. We chased the buses over seventy miles to the small town of Marion. On the way I discreetly changed into my formal attire while driving forty-five miles per hour. Comes with the territory.

The buses stopped at the city hall in Marion, but no one got off. Cops were swarming the area, so I parked away from the action and sneaked around to see what was up. I turned the corner and spotted Kaplan getting busted by a cop. He had apparently tried to board one of the buses and blend in with the crowd when an officer spotted him. The cop questioned Kaplan extensively, searched through his belongings for possible weapons, and pulled out two spy cameras, one large camera, eight rolls of film, and a cellular phone. Kaplan was told point-blank to "get the hell out of the area or get in the squad car."

Kaplan opted for the former.

I stayed around and waited for the buses to take off. It wasn't until later that evening that I found out why the buses had stopped. A city hall official had opened the office to type up the marriage license especially for Lyle and Julia.

The buses stayed around for about twenty minutes, and I used the time to call the editor and let him know what was happening. When I saw the buses start to pull away, I frantically dashed to my car and tried to follow them, but it was too late. They were long gone. I immediately panicked at the thought that I had severely screwed up the job. I called another paparazzo named Brian who was on his way to the site and asked if he knew where the buses had gone. He assured me that Larry had followed them to a church about three miles from city hall and that the wedding was taking place there.

We still didn't know if it was Julia who was getting married, for she was nowhere to be seen. As I arrived at the St. James Lutheran church, I saw buses parked outside and a phalanx of cop cars blocking the entrance to the church. If we wanted to get into the wedding, we would have to be creative.

We met up with a third photographer who had just tried to get into the wedding by saying he was invited, but of course, the cops told him to get lost.

Now it was my turn.

I drove up to the entrance and said in my sweetest voice, "My husband is in the church, and I'm late for the wedding. I just flew in from Los Angeles, and I'm supposed to meet him inside."

A cop peered through my car window and checked out the contents of my back seat. Clothes, books, tapes, and sneakers were scattered all over the place, but there was nothing that would give me away as being a reporter.

"Who's your husband?" snarled the officer.

"Jonathan Moskowitz," I answered confidently.

The cop turned to a man walking toward the church and yelled, "Marty! Do you know a Jonathan Moskowitz?"

Marty thought for a second, then shook his head no. I felt an intense urge to escape. "I think your 'husband' is driving up the hill right now," growled the cop, pointing to the photographer's car going up the hill. I looked away, threw the car in reverse, and floored it.

For the next hour, the photographers and I sat around a parking lot, trying to come up with a decent plan of action. After some intense brainstorming, we came up with the brilliant idea of just waiting around the grounds until the wedding was over, then trying to talk with the guests.

Fans were already lining up outside the church grounds, trying to get in on the hottest action to take place since the local high school basketball team won the state championship five years back. I spoke with a few fans who had heard the same rumor I had—that Julia and Lyle were indeed getting married. I couldn't believe it. I would have bet a thousand bucks that this story was bogus.

At around five o'clock, people started coming out of the church. The paparazzi, being the bloodhounds they are, smelled their prey and went in for the kill. I, on the other hand, stayed in my car and waited to follow Julia and Lyle to their next destination. I had already spoken to some of the church neighbors and to the organ player from the wedding and had gotten a fair share of details, but the most important thing was getting a photo of the newlyweds. I knew Lyle was performing that evening at the Deer Creek Music Center, only a few miles from the church, and assumed he and Julia would go straight to the Music Center since his concert started at seven o'clock and it was already close to six.

As the guests filed out of the church, the drivers positioned the buses so no one could see who was getting on. A few photographers were lucky enough to snap photos of River Phoenix, Susan Sarandon, Tim Robbins, and Michael Bolton. A few were lucky enough to get a shot of Julia and Lyle walking to their limo. Julia was barefoot, wearing only a sheer white Comme Des Garçons slip gown, and Lyle was dressed in a black tuxedo. A bodyguard held an umbrella over Julia to shield her from the rain. Even as it started to pour, no one moved off the lawn. Fans were determined to get a glimpse of Julia and her new hubby, even if they got soaked.

Because there were three limos parked behind the church, it was hard to tell which one Julia and Lyle got on. We decided to nix following them and go straight to the

Music Center, where Kaplan scalped two third-row tickets for sixty bucks a pop. We had to figure out where to put his cameras so security wouldn't notice them. Kaplan decided to stuff his small camera and two rolls of film down his pants, which looked ridiculous, and I put the large camera in my purse. There were big signs all over the concert grounds that said NO CAMERAS ALLOWED but we ignored them and took our seats.

When the lights went down, Lyle and his Large Band came on stage and the audience went wild. Seconds later, Julia walked on, still wearing her wedding gown, and the crowd continued to cheer. They started shouting her name and waving their hands in the air. She seductively kissed Lyle on the lips, then turned to the audience and said, "Ladies and gentlemen, I'd like to introduce my new husband, Lyle Lovett, and his Large Band." She kissed him once more before making her way off the stage.

Kaplan was so stunned when Julia came on stage that he forgot to put film in his camera. By the time he got it loaded, she was gone. He had missed a perfect photo opportunity that could have made him thousands of dollars, and he was pissed. The camera in my bag wasn't yet loaded, and it would have been too risky to take it out, especially since there were security guards standing at the end of each aisle, watching the crowd closely.

We both prayed that Julia would come on stage again and kiss Lyle. The tabloid gods must have heard us, because shortly thereafter Julia snuck up behind Lyle as he sang "Stand By Your Man." She wrapped her arms provocatively around his waist and rested her head on his shoulder. Kaplan went crazy. He stood up, as everyone else did, and started taking shots with his minicamera.

The audience went mad and began applauding loudly. When the song was over, Julia and Lyle kissed for a full minute and Kaplan got it all on film. As the audience sat down, I noticed two security guards looking suspiciously at Kaplan. I whispered to him that he should rewind the film quickly and give it to me, but he brushed my request off as paranoia and told me not to worry. Something inside of me knew that the security guards had seen him and that they were going to confiscate his camera.

"Give me the film," I insisted. "I know what I'm talking about."

This time he chose to trust my advice and rewound the film. I swiftly shoved the roll in my bra. A minute later, two security guards came charging down the aisle just as Kaplan was loading new film into the camera. They told him to get up and come with them but said nothing to me. I assume they didn't know we were together. As Kaplan walked away, I saw him stealthily turn the flash off on his camera and start pressing the shoot button, so that when the security guards confiscated the film, they would think they got the finished roll of Julia, not the new roll he had just loaded. I felt a rush of excitement through my body at the mere thought that I had accomplished a wonderful feat—I had saved Kaplan's film.

Thank God I was wearing a bra that night.

An hour later, Kaplan came back without his camera. They had confiscated it until the end of the show and had taken out his film, which was not to be returned. I was ex- hilarated that we had gotten enough photos to satisfy the editors at the *Enquirer.*

We went back to the hotel and as I entered my room, the thought of eating an enormous chicken salad with extra vegetables entered my mind. It was the first time in twenty- four hours that I had allowed myself to think about food, but it was almost one in the morning, too late to order room service. I opted for a fluffy pillow and soft covers and al- lowed myself to dream about food for the next eight hours.

I was awakened at 10 o'clock the next morning by fellow reporter Ed Susman, who informed me that it was time for us to find some photos of the actual wedding because the *Enquirer* was offering $25,000 and up for shots of the cere- mony. Later, in a cafe, a woman who looked to be in her fifties smiled and waved at me as she entered the restaurant with an older man. I went up to her and asked if she knew of anyone who took pictures at the wedding. She said everyone had to give their film to the guards along with their names and addresses. The film would be developed and sent to them. I thanked the woman and walked away, not thinking anything of it. I would find out later that she was none other then Lyle Lovett's mom.

The next day we heard a rumor that Julia was already on her way back to Washington, D.C., where *The Pelican Brief* was filming. But then I spoke with sources at the hotel who said they had just seen Julia eating breakfast at the cafe only an hour earlier. I had to confirm whether she and Lyle were still at the hotel. I decided to call their room. To my surprise, Lyle answered the phone.

"Hello," Lyle said in his Texas drawl.

"Lyle, it's Lysa," I blurted.

"Julia's sister Lisa?" he asked.

I lied. "Yes, yes. It's Julia's sister Lisa."

"Well, how are you doing?" Lyle asked.

"Fine," I said nervously. "Is Julia there?"

"She's here. She's just having some trouble making her way to the phone. Oh, here she comes now. Take care, we'll see you soon."

As soon as I heard that famous Pretty Woman voice say hello, I slammed down the phone.

I quickly told the paparazzo that Lyle and Julia were still in their room. Kaplan set up shop in the lobby, while Brian headed for Julia's floor to stake out the room. As soon as he got off the elevator, he was approached by two of Julia's bodyguards, who were blocking the hallway to her suite. He also spotted two hotel security guards near the stairwell. Brian came back down to the lobby and told us there was no way to get a photo on her floor because of the tight security.

We decided to post ourselves at different exits around the hotel. After waiting for more than an hour, I called their room again. This time there was no answer. Julia was slick and savvy when it came to getting out of hotels unnoticed, so I had a feeling that she and Lyle were long gone. I spoke to a hotel worker who confirmed that Julia and Lyle had in fact fled through the kitchen exit and jumped into a limousine.

The reporters and I spent five hours putting together a ten-page story of the events that had taken place over the past three days. When we were done, I went back to my room, ordered a four-course meal, and went to sleep. The next day I was told the story was over and I was free to leave. I packed my things, got into my car, and spontaneously decided to do the three-hour drive to Chicago. I felt high as a kite. The editors at the *Enquirer* were singing my name in praise.

The Roberts-Lovett story was one of the highlights of my career as a reporter. Your mind goes into overdrive when you're put under intense pressure for a short period of time, unable to eat, sleep, or shower until you've got the job done. And when it's over, food tastes wonderful, lying in bed is equivalent to floating on clouds, and standing in a shower feels like you're under a cascading waterfall in the Caribbean.

90210 to the Looney Bin

When I worked the Shannen Doherty wedding, the stress and exhaustion made me think I had lost my mind. I was the first reporter on the scene, but when reporters from "Inside Edition" showed up, Shannen threatened to shoot us all with her 9 mm handgun and tried to sic her puppy on us. The tiny little German shepherd just wagged its tail happily, so Shannen kicked the dog till it yelped.

Guests came through the gates one by one to stand around the pool in the backyard. Off-duty cops hired to provide security kept anyone from climbing the hill that overlooked Shannen's Hollywood Hills home. One paparazzo, a hirsute, malodorous Texan named E.L. Woody, was so obnoxious the reporters were begging the cops to beat him up.

I was at the scene until well after 3 A.M., trying to talk to people as they left. The next day, I was back out there before 10 A.M., waiting for Shannen to embark on her honeymoon. I tried to tail her and Ashley Hamilton as they drove off in her Porsche, but all Ashley had to do was floor it when going uphill and he left me far behind in the dust.

I slept for a total of about four hours over the next three days. By Monday, I was infiltrating the "Beverly Hills, 90210" set with Alan Zanger, crawling through the bushes on the side of a canyon in 105-degree heat so Zanger could get shots of Shannen kissing the actor who played her new boyfriend on the show. We had to crouch for hours in the blazing sun and then spring through thorns and bushes to get close enough for a shot.

I got paged and was ordered to come into the office to write up the story. I was reeling on my feet, hoping that at last I would get a break. No such luck. I had to write the story right then and there, because that same night, I was supposed to get on the red-eye to New York City to tail Shannen as she rehearsed for her appearance on "Saturday Night Live."

I had barely enough time to throw some clothes in a suitcase and change out of my dusty, filthy shirt and jeans before I had to rush to the airport. On the way, I discovered that I still had pieces of brush stuck in my hair.

Photographer Jim Knowles and I were holding plane tickets that had cost about $3,000 apiece because they had been bought at the last minute. We were to board the flight only if Shannen got on. Waiting by the gate was every other paparazzo in town, plus camera crews from the local TV stations and TV tabs. Jim and I decided to board the plane to make sure that she hadn't already got on and was hiding out in a lavatory.

Just as the door was about to close, Jim and I were

grabbing our gear to get off when I heard a flight attendant say, "She's going to get on. We're going to pull away from the gate. They'll bring up a stairway, and that way she'll avoid all the TV cameras."

"We gotta' stay, Jim," I whispered. "Everyone else is going to miss it. We're going to be heroes."

Never have I been more wrong.

The plane pulled away from the gate and stopped. The head steward was embroiled in a heated screaming match with someone on the phone. He slammed it down and said, "Fuck it. We take off now."

Shannen had demanded that everyone be ejected from first class so she could sit up there alone. Besides us tabloid bozos, there were wealthy lawyers and Japanese business-men sitting in first class who would not take kindly to this expression of celebrity pique. The head steward had re-fused to comply, and Shannen was taking another flight. Jim and I were trapped on the plane.

We looked like fools.

It got worse.

We arrived at JFK airport only to find that Doherty was going to land at Newark. We were supposed to meet a grungy New York paparazzo who would drive us there to get a shot of her and her hubby getting off the plane. The paparazzo took off without us. We called him back and drove to Newark like maniacs, only to miss Shannen and Ashley.

Again.

I was so tired by this point that I was stumbling around in a dreamlike state. When we were ordered to go to the Paramount Hotel, I was elated, thinking that at last I would get to slack off.

Nope. Shannen and her husband were holed up in their room at the Paramount, and we were ordered, ON PAIN OF INSTANT DEATH, not to miss the shot of her leaving the hotel to go to the "Saturday Night Live" studio. It was Tuesday, the day we "lock up" the magazine, the absolute last day we could get a picture in. The editors were holding space for it, and dammit, they wanted something to fill it.

One paparazzo managed to get us a room just down the hall from Shannen, but the manager ordered us out because the room had already been reserved. We barricaded the door against security, but they shoved it open and dragged us out by our hair.

Out on the sidewalk, we had reporters and photographers stationed at every exit of the hotel.

Shannen came out through a secret door leading to a deli.

We missed the shot again.

I held the phone five inches from my ear and I still got a headache from the screaming. The Star *was assigning another team. Fine. I just wanted to crawl into a hole.*

The next morning, I awoke in my room at the Paramount, decorated in billowing white fabrics and shiny stainless steel. Because I had been so tired, I woke up in a kind of fugue state. My mind was fuzzy. I was still half asleep, and it seemed like I was in a really vivid dream. Then I looked around at my antiseptic surroundings and the first thought I had was: Oh my God, I've lost my mind, and they've locked me away.

I glanced out the window and saw New York, but I had no idea where I was or how I had gotten there.

I was terrified. It wasn't until I found the messages we had bribed a maid to steal from Shannen's room earlier that I remembered where I was.

Double-dealing Nuptials
East Hampton, New York
August 1993

Whenever two major celebrities tie the knot, tab editors go crazy. The same goes for divorces, births, and deaths. The bigger the celebrity is, the more money the tabloids make.

But when I told David Perel, the Florida editor at the *Enquirer,* about Kim Basinger and Alec Baldwin's wedding, he seemed only casually interested. He asked me where the event was taking place and if my source could get into the wedding. I told him all the details of the event, thinking that I would be sent to New York to cover it, which was standard procedure for a reporter who comes up with a lead. Little did I know what a con artist Perel was. He tried to get me to believe that my information wasn't worth very much so that I would readily feed him everything I knew. Basinger and Baldwin were keeping the address a secret until the last minute, even from their closest friends.

As the day of the wedding drew closer, I asked Perel if I was going to be covering the story. He said no, giving me some lame excuse that it cost less for them to send a reporter from Florida than from California.

What a crock!

Money was not the issue and the *Enquirer* knew it; the issue was trust. They wanted to send a correspondent who had been with the magazine a long time, someone whom they could control better than me. They wanted to be sure the reporter wouldn't pocket the *Enquirer*'s money, then sell the story to the *Star,* robbing the *Enquirer* of an exclusive. Up to that point, I had never double-crossed a magazine, so they had no reason to doubt my loyalty. Through the grapevine I learned that Perel had made a deal with the reporter he did send: They would sell my story to the Brits, Australians, and anyone else who would dish out the dough. Perel didn't know me well enough to make such a deal with me, so I was left either to stop working for him or to bite it and deliver the goods. I chose the latter, but not without a fight.

"I gave you the lead!" I shouted at Perel. "And don't give me a song-and-dance about it being cheaper to send someone from Florida than California. Money is not the issue here, and you know it!"

He was silent. No quick comebacks or fierce words to

make me feel small. He knew I was right, but he was in charge and I had to live with that. Editors and senior reporters are a skanky bunch. They stick together like glue and are often the ones stealing the most money from the papers, which overpay them to start. They have worked for the tabloids long enough to know every trick of the trade, and when they're given a golden opportunity to make a quick buck, they'll take it.

I had too much at stake to mess with the enemy. I relied on the money from my stories to pay my bills. I was not in a position to be cocky and threaten to sell my story elsewhere. The truth was, my only other connection was with the *Star,* but if I went to them, I would be finished working for the *Enquirer* for good.

"Listen," David said softly. "You're still going to work on the story. You will get paid for the lead and for your time, but we need one of our staffers to cover the actual event. We're sending one of your sources anyway, so you'll write up everything he tells you. These aren't my rules, they're the *Enquirer*'s rules."

He went on jerking my chain until I finally interrupted and said it was okay, that I would work on the story from home.

My source was freaking out about going to the wedding and getting details and photos without being found out. He happened to be close friends with one of the Baldwin brothers, so getting caught selling a story to the rags would have definitely ended their friendship. From the moment he left Los Angeles for New York, the entire event turned into a nightmare. First off, I didn't tell Perel that my source hadn't even been invited to the wedding. He knew the bride and groom well enough, but without an invitation he probably wouldn't get past the front door. This of course would put me in deep water because the *Enquirer* was forking out money to send my source in the hopes he'd get a killer shot.

Then, to my dismay, the day before the nuptials, the *New York Post* printed a story stating where and when the wedding was going to take place. The exclusivity of my story was blown, and so was my bargaining power. Luckily, my source didn't have any problem getting into the wedding, and I was relieved because he would be able to get exclusive details about the event itself.

Wrong.

Somehow more details leaked out to the press, and my source became less and less valuable. The only thing that would save me now was if he got an exclusive photo of Kim and Alec. I asked Perel how much that photo would be worth to the *Enquirer* and he answered, "Not much, but they would want it anyway."

I was tired of being put down, swindled, and manipulated by this obnoxious, nasal-voiced toad, so I decided to do something about it.

I called the *Star.*

Double-dealing is a very big no-no in the world of tabloid reporting, even though almost everyone does it. The quickest way to get axed is by selling the same story to more than one paper. I was pissed enough at Perel to take a chance. I phoned the *Star* and spoke with the editors. They quickly jumped at the chance to buy my information and pay my source at the same time. I told them that I would give them information the *Enquirer* didn't have, in exchange for the promise that they wouldn't reveal my double-deal to the *Enquirer. Star* bureau chief Bob Smith gave his word, so I spilled the beans.

Since the *Enquirer* had paid for my source's flight to New York as well as his hotel room, they were expecting something in return. Through a few paparazzi pals of mine, I learned the photos would be worth a bundle overseas. I quickly got the pictures from my source and lied to Perel that we were not able to come up with any shots. In the end, my source received money from both tabloids and never got found out by the Baldwins.

Unfortunately, what goes around comes around. A few days after I had paid my source the $2,500 we had agreed upon for his information, he asked to borrow $160. I loaned him the money in good faith, and he promised to pay me back in one week. Three months later, I received a check from him.

It bounced.

Tarantulas, Liz Taylor, and Hot-air Balloons
Santa Ynez, California
October 1991

Before I joined the Star, *Liz Taylor had always been an anachronistic joke to me, best symbolized by John Belushi's razor-edged "Saturday Night Live" parody of her as a bloated monstrosity, choking on a chicken bone and giving herself the Heimlich maneuver.*

Since then, I've learned the American public has an almost endless appetite for the personal life of this poor, hounded woman. Worse, the fascination seems to be shared by almost every western democracy, where exclusive pictures of Liz doing anything brings tens of thousands of dollars. The competition for even insignificant scraps of information about her life is ferocious.

In 1990, I narrowly missed taking a picture of Liz as she was evacuated from Harbor Medical Hospital because her pneumonia was beyond what the staff could handle. I was stationed near the front of the hospital building and photographer Alan Zanger was in a parking garage to the side. Reporter Donna Balancia spotted Larry Fortensky, Liz's then-boyfriend, driving up, followed by carloads of Israeli security. Zanger scrambled onto the roof, took the shot, retreated to his car, and was pursued for miles by security guards on motorcycles. He stuffed the film down his pants and drove like a maniac to escape. Meanwhile, I was running across the street, camera in hand, as Liz's ambulance pulled away.

Zanger's one frame of film netted him more than $300,000 in worldwide sales.

A year later, Liz announced she was getting married. In the Star *newsroom, we all groaned. It was going to be hell.*

A month before the ceremony, bureau chief Barry Levine and I went up to Santa Ynez to check out Michael Jackson's Neverland Ranch, where the wedding was going to take place. We wanted to scout out the best way to get in there unnoticed. After checking into a hotel in nearby Santa Barbara, we set out.

Jackson's place is just about impregnable. It's in a bowl-shaped valley, invisible from the highway, surrounded by high hills devoid of cover. The grounds allegedly have three tiers of security: motion detectors, seismic sensors, and laser beams. Plus, Jackson was hiring every off-duty Santa Barbara County sheriff's deputy available and trucking in hundreds of private security guards.

It was the end of the day, the sun was setting, and the temperature was dropping. As we drove along the back side of the ranch, looking for dirt roads that led into the hills, we noticed strange black objects skittering across the blacktop. We cruised past one that was the size of a dinner plate. It looked like it had eight legs.

"Barry? I think that was a tarantula."

"What? No way."

We rounded a curve and the road in front of us seemed to writhe from the sheer black mass of huge tarantulas scuttling around. We both screamed and rolled up the windows. Apparently we had chosen to do our recon during tarantula breeding season. The entire way back to Santa Barbara, we kept checking under the seats to make sure none of them had managed to get into the car.

With such intense, high-tech layers of security in place at Neverland, it was obvious there was no way we were going to be able to sneak in. Which left two options: Do it by air, or make it an inside job.

Luckily (I thought) we had a person on our payroll who

had been invited to the wedding. I would pose as a limo driver and drive him through the gates with a spy camera hidden in my hat, then wander away from the rest of the hired help to get a couple of shots.

As the wedding day approached, we learned that all guests would have to pass through a metal detector and then through some other kind of machine that would fog the film in any hidden cameras.

What an excellent idea. A hundred free chest X rays to every guest, whether you want them or not.

"Barry," I said, "I didn't sign up for radiation poisoning."

He grinned. "Don't sweat it. I'm sure the Star's insurance will pay for only the best toupee once your hair starts falling out. Besides, if you're glowing, you won't need a flashlight when you're sneaking through Michael's menagerie to get shots of the elephant rides."

All joking aside, we were worried. How to get a camera through? The wedding was taking place at dusk, so I'd need to use sensitive high-speed film.

Then our inside source began to get cold feet. The miserable cur. He wanted us to guarantee he wouldn't get caught. Or that we'd pay all his legal bills if he did get caught. He wanted to know how much the pictures were worth, and wanted all the money in advance. He wanted to be put up in a luxury hotel for a month before the wedding because he was so nervous he couldn't sleep at home. The guy was flaking out before our very eyes, and all chances of pulling a coup were rapidly disappearing.

It looked like we would have to take to the air.

We already knew, though, that approximately fifteen to twenty-five helicopters and pilots were to be on standby the day of the wedding, and that Liz and Michael were trying to get the Federal Aviation Administration to restrict the airspace over the ranch. Barry thought he had hit on the solution to our problems. We called it the Wizard of Oz plan: Send up a hot-air balloon. A balloon has much less

*vibration, can go lower, and moves slower than a heli-
copter.*

*We managed to find the scurviest balloonists on the en-
tire West Coast. We quickly dubbed them Larry, Moe, and
Curly. The purported pilot was a rheumy-eyed old geezer
with a hearing aid who claimed to have cut his teeth in
balloons as an artillery observer in World War I. The leader
was a bald-headed lump of gristle who told tales of dubious
exploits in Florida's Everglades, where he was apparently
an expert at using a cutting torch to take metal gates off
their hinges and thus gain entrance to government land.
What that had to do with ballooning, I couldn't tell.*

*Next order of business was to establish a secure base of
operations. Jackson's ranch is miles from any sort of sani-
tary facility, and it wasn't likely that we'd be welcomed
with open arms by his neighbors. It'd be more likely for
Liz's people to pay off the local ranchers to starve their pit
bulls and load their Ithaca 12-gauges with rock salt.*

*I went back to Los Angeles to put together a plan. When
I entered the* Star *office, it looked like an electronics swap
meet. There were mounds of cell phones, walkie-talkies,
parabolic microphones, night-vision goggles, and radio
scanners. That was when I learned my role in our little
drama had changed. I was now to be in charge of getting
the balloon in the air. Reporter Kate Caldwell would ride
in it, along with a photographer with more guts (or love of
spectacle) than brains. Then I was to try to infiltrate, using
whatever methods necessary, and either observe the scene
or take photos.*

*On the eve of the big day, Liz was scheduled to have a
pre-wedding dinner party at the Los Olivos Grand Hotel,
about fifteen miles down the road from the Jackson ranch.
It would be the only time during the entire weekend that
Liz would come out from behind Neverland's razor wire. It
would probably be our best chance to get a decent shot of
her, if not our only chance.*

The hotel dining room had three entrances. Even though

we had about nine people, including two photographers and a photo editor from New York, we still couldn't get a shot of her. As we skimmed over a hastily sketched battle plan on the hood of Barry's car, a family who lived near the hotel approached us. They were curious and wanted to know where we were from. Reacting with customary paranoia, Barry forbade us to talk to them, figuring they were plants from Liz's security team sent to ferret out our plan of action. Puzzled by our reticence, they brought out a cooler full of beer and tried to make peace.

A half hour later, all suspicions were forgotten, and the family had become part of our crack Star magazine assault team. We issued them cameras and stationed them strategically around the hotel. They relished their roles. Like most people, the opportunity to get involved in something big and important proved to be irresistible.

I looked up from where I was stationed and saw a long string of lights coming down Foxen Canyon Road. "Here they come," I radioed to Barry. Instantly, the radio was filled with excited yelps from the photogs and they asked me all at once where the cars were headed. One by one the limos arrived at the front of the hotel and celebs got out. Our team and the rest of the press started filtering to the entrance to see who was arriving, sure that they were going to miss something or someone. Suddenly Barry started screaming, "They're going in on the side. Everyone get here now! They're going in on the side!"

I took off toward the side entrance. Apparently Liz's security had sneaked a limo around the main drag and, with a Winnebago shielding the door from the paparazzi, pulled right up to the side entrance and unloaded Liz. She had slipped inside, right under our noses.

Barry was in a rage, kicking in the side panels of my truck. A throng of cursing photogs tried to get up on the porch and peer through the curtained windows. Cursing security men pushed them back. Accusations and recriminations were everywhere.

Well, now that she was in, we weren't going to be fooled again. She would not be allowed to get out. About a hundred paparazzi and fifteen TV crews settled in for protracted trench warfare. The townie family we had met looked around blankly, then began taking pictures of one another and the rest of the media. Barry confiscated their cameras for wasting film.

About every five minutes, Barry would radio me and demand to know if I was at the side and if I had seen anything. "Still here and nothing going on," I would say as calmly as I could.

"Test the flash. Make sure it works."

"I already tested it. It works."

"Test it again."

"All that does is run down the batteries."

"Then change the batteries. I want to know if it works."

I took seven pictures of the pavement that night.

We waited until well past 11 P.M. for Liz to come out. All the other guests had left by nine. They told us Liz had left before they did. Hotel staff came out and said the same. We didn't believe them. All the security guards pulled out. They told us Liz was long gone. We didn't believe them, either.

Liz had indeed left, through a boarded-up door, which led to the locked and darkened post office, which led to a store, which led to an office, which led to a door onto a side street. We had been fooled again.

Barry was inconsolable. "This is not a good sign," he sighed wearily as he tossed half-full water bottles and film canisters into his cluttered backseat. "Tomorrow I want you all up at the crack of dawn."

The next morning I got up, went outside to my truck, and began blasting Wagner's "Ride of the Valkyries." Kate, Bev, Barry, and Bob were doubled over laughing. Larry, Moe, and Curly looked at us blankly. These guys are going to be a barrel of laughs, *I thought.*

Things kept getting weirder. Weeks earlier, Barry had tossed off a line in a story about how uncouth the Fortenskys

*were going to be at the reception. It went something like:
"While most of the Hollywood hotshots will be feasting on
paté, caviar, and Dom Perignon, Larry's relatives will be
asking if they can get some Kentucky Fried Chicken and a
Coke."*

*Some eager young advertising executive at KFC saw the
line and decided to jump on the bandwagon. They came up
to our cars with a roach coach stocked to the roof with
honey-coated KFC and a big banner that read* KFC WANTS TO
CONGRATULATE THE FORTENSKYS FOR THEIR TASTE IN WOMEN . . .
AND FOOD. *They started laying out dozens of trays of barbecued chicken. I was gnawing a wing and dripping grease
on Barry's keyboard when he ordered me out of the mobile
trailer and told me to help Curly find a spot to put up the
balloon.*

*We had two hours until Liz walked down the aisle, and
our search for a launching pad was looking more and more
iffy. At times, the truck was hub-deep in loose mud. I had
visions of being attacked by tarantulas. Finally we found an
unguarded gate that led to a cow pasture that led to . . . a
Texaco oil patch. Big grasshoppers thrummed up and
down hypnotically amid holding tanks. Small puddles of
crude oil soaked the thick, dry grass. The smell of flamma-
ble petrochemicals was heavy in the air. But there was
more than enough room to set up the balloon, and the wind
was blowing in the right direction, as conveniently indi-
cated by the swaying barrage balloons Jackson had put up
to hinder the choppers.*

*Curly and I drove back to the command post to pick up
John Ecker, who would be helping us with the heavy lifting;
Kate, who was in the midst of giving a gung-ho interview
to other TV tabs; and the photog. Curly ran over to where
the other two stooges sat picking their noses and began gesticulating wildly.*

Kate was saying, "Yes, the crack Star *team has been in
training for this assault for the last three months in the Te-
hachapis with the help of the Navy SEALs. We've been*

studying aeronautics and cliff rappelling, living and eating with some of this country's toughest soldiers . . ."

The barbecued chicken seemed to have attracted swarms of bees, and the cooks were waving their grill forks wildly and coughing amid clouds of black smoke. Four carloads of paparazzi were lined up for the free eats, licking their chops.

Inside the trailer, all hell was breaking loose. Cell phones were ringing, the walkie-talkie crackled with Jennifer's updates, the map on the wall with its strategically placed pins had fallen down, and someone had spilled a liter of Coke onto the computer disks.

"Barry," I said, "they're talking about launching the balloon from the Texaco oil pumping station."

"Yeah, so? What, it's not big enough?"

"No, it's a perfect place to take off and float over the ranch. But Barry, to inflate a hot-air balloon you gotta light a giant propane torch that shoots out a thirty-foot flame. Maybe it's just me, but sparking a lighter that size in a field full of raw gasoline seems like a bad idea."

"They wouldn't do it if they didn't think it was safe."

"Barry, take a good look at those guys. They're so out of it, I doubt any of them can balance a checkbook, much less think out potentially deadly risks."

"Just get out of here, Dave."

"Okay, but if you hear a real loud noise from the south, that's us."

John and I helped Curly load a gigantic cylinder of helium into the back bed of the pickup truck. A passing Spy magazine photographer pulled over and took a picture of us hefting the big, silvery torpedo. Kate, John, and Curly hopped into the truck, and they squealed out, spraying gravel and towing a minitrailer loaded down with the deflated balloon.

I got into my truck and paused, not believing that these could be the last hours of my life, and wrote out a sour, cantankerous will, leaving my meager savings to any person who could provide the executors of my will with proof that he or she had hacked off one or all of Barry Levine's limbs.

I started up the engine and drove out to the oil patch. When I got there, I saw John and Kate rolling up the huge wad of cloth.

I leaned out the window. "Finally came to your senses, huh?"

"Yeah, check it out. The wind changed quarter," Kate said. "We've got to go north along this road until we hit a spot where we can take off and hit the ranch. If we take off from here, we'll miss it by miles."

Made sense to me.

I followed the pickup down the road, looking for a spot where the wind would be more or less right. Curly kept inhaling the helium and talking in a squeaky voice to Kate, trying to break the tension with a routine that must have gone over like a charm.

"Knock it off, man," Kate snarled. "We're professionals."

Not long after, Barry was on the radio, flipping out. The guests were assembling under the pavilions, and the choppers were in the air.

But where were we?

In deep shit, that's where.

With no time to spare, we settled on the gravel shoulder of a stretch of road barely big enough for our cars. The photographer's girlfriend had also come along, and I gave her a video camera to record what I suspected would be the last time he would be able to walk without assistance. Then the Stooges put John and me to work doing all the heavy lifting.

I quickly found out that balloon fabric stinks like rancid goat. And for something the FAA classifies as lighter than air, it weighs a ton. John and I were sweating and running around in a frenzy as the Stooges set up a giant fan to blow air into the bag and get it partially inflated before they turned on the torch. Kate and John and I had to grab the guylines to keep the balloon in one place. Meanwhile, the old coots leaned against the tailgate and jacked their jaws. I was starting to steam because we were doing all the work, but now that we were out of the oil patch, I wasn't going to bitch too much.

After about fifteen minutes, we had the balloon at almost life size. Then the wind started to swirl. The balloon began to dribble like a basketball. We couldn't hold it, and the old bastards just stood there and watched as this big balloon kicked our asses. It would lift up into the air, hesitate, then smack back down to earth. It was bouncing out over the road, blocking both lanes of traffic. I felt like I was riding a bucking bronco. I was getting lifted ten feet into the air, then dropped hard. A couple of times I had to crawl through the gravel to avoid getting steamrolled. On the other side of the balloon, Kate screamed in fear as the balloon lifted her up and over the cliff, dangling her feet over a hundred-foot drop.

Suddenly the fan cut out. The three idiots walked inside the balloon, looking worried. The balloon had snagged on a previously unnoticed barbed wire fence, and a five-foot-long hole had been ripped in its side. "Can you patch it?" I asked them.

"Not a hole that big," Moe answered. He yanked the cord that opened the Velcro vents and deflated the whole thing. Rolling the balloon up was even more work than pulling it out.

Sweaty, dirty, bruised, and exhausted, I walked back to my truck. Barry was yelling, "It's going down right now!" on the radio, and Jim was reporting from his hovering chopper, "I'm getting a photo of Taylor. She's with Jackson."

I got on the radio. "Barry, we've had an accident."

"Nobody got hurt, did they?" he asked.

"Not for lack of trying. The balloon's got a big-ass hole in it, and they can't patch it and they don't have a spare."

"Get back here then, and let's get our $2,000 back."

I walked over to the morons and said, "Let's go back to the command post."

I arrived at the trailer in five minutes. The Three Stooges showed up, dumped off Kate, and took off, peeling rubber, Curly at the wheel.

"Get my two thousand back!" screamed Ira Berger, Star's photo editor.

John and I took off in Bev's car.

At one point we almost chucked it all to go to a bar and get shit-faced. We never did catch up with the balloon bozos and went back to the command post in defeat.

By this time the wedding was long over, and Jim in the chopper was radioing in to say he had gotten photos of Liz and Larry walking down the aisle, of them on the altar, and of the gonzo parachutist who landed fifteen feet from them. He also mentioned that he had thrown out his back and was heading directly back to L.A. for treatment. I headed straight for the abandoned trays of KFC chicken, by now covered with ants and bees.

They tasted good.

6

RULES OF THE GAME

1. If a celebrity is seen holding hands with or kissing a person of the opposite sex (relatives and children not included), they are "dating."
2. As soon as the couple moves in together, they are attempting "a trial marriage."
3. A few months after they get married, there is "trouble in the relationship."
4. If problems persist, they're headed for "a divorce."
5. Once divorced, if they are seen holding hands with or kissing a person of the opposite sex, they are "dating."

And so, the cycle begins anew.

As a tabloid reporter, one of the most common questions people asked me was, "Are the stories you write true?" to which I replied, "Yes and no." Tabloid reporters can't outright lie about something or else we'd get sued. But there's always room for embellishment. Enormous room.

If a celebrity was in love, I'd use words like *madly, intensely,* and *passionately* when describing his or her feelings. If someone close to a celebrity had just died or a star was going through a divorce, I'd write sentences like, "Tears welled up in her eyes as she saw her husband leave their house for the last time," or "The pain ran so deep that she couldn't utter a word at the funeral." Basically, tabloids want the copy to sound like a trashy novel.

But I couldn't just write that Tom Cruise had some life-threatening illness if I didn't have proof either in the form of a confession from Cruise himself, from his medical records, or from an extremely reliable source like his wife or mother. The "dangerous" stories that lawyers have a field day "vetting" are ones that involve diseases, sexual preferences, drug use, insanity, and infidelity. Lying about these things not only is prohibited but spells "instant lawsuit" for the paper.

Sometimes, though, lawsuits come out of seemingly innocent stories, ones in which all the facts are true, but the celebrity being written about just doesn't like the way he or she was portrayed in the copy. Such was the case with Rodney Dangerfield. In August of 1990, Dangerfield was suing Caesars Palace in Las Vegas because his eye was burned by the scalding water in a hot tub. The hotel claimed that the injury was his fault, that he was high on drugs at the time, had drank too much booze, and was careless.

David was sent to cover the story, and what emerged from speaking with numerous sources at the hotel was a dark picture of a comedian who had little self-esteem and a lot of problems. Again and again, sources claimed they'd seen Rodney high on drugs, acting obnoxiously.

Dangerfield managed to win the lawsuit against Caesars for a cool sum of $250,000, after which he decided to sue the *Star* for running the story. He won again, but this time the sum was a paltry $45,000, 40 percent of which went to his lawyers.

Most celebrities decide that suing is not worth the hassle, time, or inconvenience. They'll choose to write off or laugh at a story rather than make it the focus of their lives. A lawsuit can take up to five years to settle, and even then the chances of winning may not outweigh the legal costs involved.

David was dragged into a lawsuit when Peter Criss of the band Kiss sued the *Star* for mistaken identity. A homeless man in Venice, California, had called the *Star* claiming that he was Peter Criss. David was used to dealing with wackos, but he decided to give this guy a chance to prove himself and set up an interview.

He and photographer Julian Wasser met the guy on the lawn of the Santa Monica courthouse, and David compared him to a faxed photograph he had of the real Criss. Even though the guy was dressed in smelly rags, a grungy baseball hat, and sneakers with holes in them, David and Julian both agreed that he might be for real. Furthermore, the guy was wearing an ID bracelet on his wrist from St. John's Hospital that said "Peter Criss." David asked the man for some more ID, and the guy promptly handed him a library card, a hospital bill, a prescription for Lasix, and a piece of stationery, all of which bore the name Peter Criss. After gathering facts and background on the guy, David relayed it to bureau chief Barry Levine, who told him to go ahead with the story.

Star paid to put "Criss" in a hotel and gave him a couple hundred bucks to clean himself up. The story he relayed to David was that he had been distraught ever since his band had broken up, that he had lost his family and his friends, and that he was facing a life of hopelessness and destitution on Venice beach.

As David listened to the man's woes, he had a bad feeling; something just didn't sit right. Then things got complicated. Roseanne and Tom Arnold decided to save "Criss." They bought him meals and promised to get him into rehab. Old Kiss fans showed up to get him to sign autographs and sing his old hit songs. A story about how Tom and Roseanne were helping the bum ran the following week. And then the shit hit the fan.

The *Star* received a letter from lawyers of the real Peter Criss, stating that he was suing the magazine for $50 million for defamation of character, pain and suffering, and a host of other complaints. As the trial date drew near, David became terrified at the thought of being cross-examined in front of a television camera for all of America to see. He knew the trial would attract a lot of news and television coverage, coverage he could do without. Once you were sued, you were a marked reporter in the eyes of reputable publications.

Minutes before David was set to take the witness stand, Criss and the *Star* settled out of court for an undisclosed amount. The impostor mysteriously disappeared, never to be heard from again.

Most stories are okay to elaborate and embellish upon. Most people don't sue over the good things you write about them, so embellishing on their happiness and joy is usually a safe call.

Bob Smith once sent me on a mission to find a former Miss America who had confessed that her boyfriend used to beat her up, and she was finally ready to speak out about her ordeal. Bob gave me her "so-called" address and sent me to her apartment to get an interview. When I first read the address, I thought he was kidding because the apartment was located in one of the worst neighborhoods in Los Angeles. Logic told me that a beautiful, white former Miss America who had just gotten out of an abusive relationship wouldn't be living in a ghetto, and I wasn't about to risk my life to find out if she did. To keep Bob happy, I told him I'd check out the address, but instead of going downtown, I caught an afternoon movie. I phoned Bob after the film ended and told him the address didn't belong to the woman. Ironically, a week later Bob came up with the right address, which was a beautiful condo located in the Hollywood Hills.

Tony Frost, the bureau chief for the *Enquirer*, once called me up at 10 P.M. and asked me to go to a house located deep in the hills of Santa Monica. The assignment was to go to the house and wait until someone came home. He told me not to get noticed under any circumstances, which meant I had to sit in my car with the lights off and motor stopped. I thought it was an easy enough assignment in exchange for a quick 150 bucks. I drove down the dark, dirt road for over a mile and finally spotted the large, Spanish-style mansion. I drove around a few times, looking for possible license plates or signs of life in the house, but there were none. There were also no lights on the street, so when I turned off my car and sat outside the house, everything was pitch black. I felt like I was in one of those low-budget horror films where the girl is necking with her boyfriend in their convertible when all of the sudden a madman bursts through the window and kills them both. I sat in the car for approximately three minutes until I scared myself adequately to bag the assignment and tell Tony I had waited there for hours and hadn't seen a thing.

He believed me.

In February of '94, David was told to work on a story about Mary Wilson of The Supremes. She had gotten in a harrowing car accident when she fell asleep at the wheel, crashing the car and killing her teenaged son in the process. When David was assigned to the story, Wilson was at the hospital in a coma. She had not yet heard that her son was dead and the *Star* wanted David to be the one to tell her. They were interested in seeing her reaction as she came out of the coma and heard that her young son was gone.

David was disgusted with the assignment, but went to the hospital anyway. He didn't get near Wilson and was relieved when her family came to tell her the bad news instead of having to do it himself.

Most of the time, the assignments I went on were exciting, challenging, and fun. They often made me feel like a private detective, trying to track down a star or put clues together to make sense of a story. Once in a while an assignment was sleazy, and I had to try and do the best I could without losing too much sleep. In those cases, I would leave the assignment early, try and skirt the issue, or bag it altogether if I thought there was no chance of getting the assignment done.

Some reporters had no shame about sneaking into a funeral to interview the guests or about following a celebrity around to catch them in an extramarital affair. It was a thrill to these reporters; the thrill of the chase and the rush of the catch. I used to feel that adrenaline pump through me when I followed a celeb in a high-speed chase or when I spotted a star in the middle of a crowd. But as with any great high, a low usually follows.

Bar Crawling for Kidman
Los Angeles, California
April 1993

The assignment was this: Go to a lesbian bar to look for a major celebrity's wife and her "new" girlfriend.

A week before I was sent to look for Tom Cruise's wife, Nicole Kidman, at the exclusive lesbian club called She-Bar, a source of mine had spotted Shannen Doherty dancing the night away at the same posh club. Shannen had gotten up on stage and danced with other women, rubbing her body up close against theirs.

Because the club moved nightly to different restaurants and bars around Los Angeles, I needed help in finding my quarry. She-Bar doesn't allow straight men or women in the club, so I found myself a gal pal who was "in the know" and willing to be my date for the evening.

When we arrived at She-Bar, we had to act, look like, and make believe we were lovers, at least until we got into the club. My friend told me she had seen other supposedly "straight" female celebrities at the club, including Jodie Foster, Whitney Houston, Kelly McGillis, and Lori Petty.

As we entered the club, I immediately noticed the number of beautiful, feminine women who graced the place.

Stereotypes of lesbians went totally out the window as I came face-to-face with some of the most stunning women I'd ever laid eyes on. My pal and I took a table near the back. She wanted us to look genuine, so she started rubbing my shoulders and whispering in my ear. I told her to cut it out, that we didn't have to fawn all over each other to pass as lesbians.

Later, while we were on the dance floor, I spotted a woman with long, thick red hair, wearing a black cap, loose-fitting jeans, and a short sweater. She looked exactly like Kidman from the back. Even her height matched the sexy star's height. Adrenaline started to pump as I slithered toward her, slyly taking my camera out of my purse as I prepared to get a shot of Kidman in action. As I came closer, it became apparent she was not Kidman. I began to think the entire lead was a fluke, that Nicole had never been spotted, and my source was mistaken.

Almost every big star has been accused of being a closet homosexual or lesbian or, at the very least, bisexual. I once got a job working for a newly–formed gay cable station. At our first creative meeting, the topic was Tom Cruise's sexuality. All of the gay men in the room swore to me Tom was gay. They said they knew people who had slept with him. Other male celebrities who have been rumored to be gay include Tom Selleck, Richard Gere, Keanu Reeves, and Matt Dillon. These men are among the hunks of Hollywood, and their images would be greatly tarnished if it came out that the rumors were true. Even though their chances of meeting or dating a star are remote, fans still like to fantasize that they are the woman their favorite male celebrity is passionately embracing.

If my unsuccessful Nicole Kidman hunt is any indication, and big celebs like Cruise are indeed keeping their sexual preference a secret, they're sure doing a good job of it.

My So-Called Life with Oprah
Los Angeles, California, and Chicago, Illinois
December 1993

Oprah Winfrey.

What do you think of when you see that name? Megarich
TV talk-show host? Yo-yo dieter? Marriage-phobic woman
who courageously told the world she was sexually abused
as a child? The name Oprah Winfrey brings up so many
different images. She has found success despite enormous
odds and has risen to the top of her field.

I sought out Oprah Winfrey at the end of 1993. I had
quit working exclusively for the *Star* and had been freelancing for the *Enquirer.* Although I still enjoyed the money
and excitement that working for the tabloids brought, I
needed a change. Because I was creative and innovative
when it came to developing stories, I thought I'd be good
as a talk-show producer. Oprah was my favorite, so I sent
out my résumé and deliberately left out the fact that I had
worked for the tabloids.

Three months later, I received a phone call from one of
Oprah's assistants, explaining that they wanted me to fly to
Chicago for an interview in two days' time. I was thrilled,
ecstatic, stunned. The next day, I received a package containing a plane ticket and information about the time and
place of my interview. Everything happened so quickly that
I didn't have time to contemplate what moving to Chicago
would entail: cold weather, big-city life, leaving my friends.
I decided to take things one day at a time and trust that
everything would work out.

From the moment I arrived in Chicago, everything
turned to shit. On the way to the studio, the cab ran into
traffic, and I ended up being late to the interview. I also left
my date and address book in the back of the cab, so I
couldn't fill out the many forms the secretary handed me,
because all the names and phone numbers of my contacts
were in that book. The forms contained intricate, detailed

questions, and I knew I'd have to 'fess up about working for the tabloids because they would find out during my background check if I didn't. I was stuck between a rock and a hard place. What happened next was worse than any tabloid horror story.

An assistant called me in to meet with Diane Hudson, one of the show's senior producers. The woman was cordial and professional and read my résumé slowly as I looked around the office. She smiled after reading one of my clippings and told me I was an extremely good writer. I told her a bit about myself, about my experience as a writer, and about my spiritual path as a student of *A Course in Miracles,* of which Oprah was also a student. After five minutes of chatting, Hudson asked me about some of my prior jobs. I knew my time had come. I had to 'fess up or escape. I chose the former.

"I used to work for *Star* magazine," I blurted out.

She did a double-take. "What did you say?" she asked.

"I used to work for *Star* magazine, but I quit about a year ago," I repeated.

"I can't hire you," she said flatly.

That was it. All my credentials and writing abilities went out the window because I used to work for *Star* magazine. What was she going to do when I told her I still wrote for the *National Enquirer?*

I decided to challenge her. "I freelance for the *National Enquirer.*"

"Now I definitely can't hire you. And there's no point in going on with this interview, so thank you for your time. Please leave."

I had flown two thousand miles to get smacked in the face by a woman I hardly knew. At least I got a free trip to Chicago. She waited for me to pick up my things and leave, but I wouldn't budge. I wasn't going to give up that easily.

"Let me get this straight," I uttered. "Five minutes ago, you told me I was a good writer. Great, in fact. You told me you were impressed with my work and my ability to explore the human psyche through my words. But now that you know I write for the tabloids, you think I'm not capable of changing? Once a tabloid sleaze, always a tabloid sleaze?"

"I still think you're a good writer," Hudson said. "But how can you expect me to hire you when you work for the tabloids? Oprah is in the tabloids almost every week. She's been very hurt by the harsh stories that are printed about her. How could I justify hiring you? It would be ludicrous. Say a few months down the line I found out that you secretly sold an Oprah story to the tabloids. How would I look for hiring you, knowing you had contacts with the tabs? I would look like a fool."

"But how do you know that the person you end up hiring won't also have connections with the tabloids?" I persisted. "It's not so hard to make connections. You just pick up the phone and say, 'I have a story about Oprah I want to sell,' and *poof,* instant connections. At least I told you the truth. Also, why would I want to risk moving 2,000 miles to screw myself over by selling a story about Oprah? And where do you think we get our stories from, anyway? We get them from people who work for Oprah Winfrey. People in this office. People who see her day in and day out and know what's going on in her life. I chose to tell you the truth, and now I'm being judged for it."

She wouldn't budge. In her eyes, I was rotten garbage, ready to be thrown into the gutter. We argued for a few more minutes until I finally got up and left. As I stormed out of her office, I threw down my résumé and the papers I had filled out. I ran into the bathroom and broke down crying. I realized I had gotten what I deserved. Hudson could never justify hiring an ex-tabloid reporter.

I left the studio and checked into a seedy motel. Whenever I traveled on the road for the *Star* or the *Enquirer,* I stayed in the best hotels. Now that I was picking up the tab, I had to lower my standards. The room consisted of a warped bed, a mildew-stained shower, and a medium-size TV with a fuzzy picture.

I spent the rest of the weekend schlepping around Chicago on my own, visiting museums, shopping, going to movies. I ended up having a good time despite the trip's tumultuous beginning. I had learned an important lesson: never be afraid to tell the truth about your past. If someone is going to judge you on it, then so be it. You cannot change the choices you made. You are what you are, dirty laundry and all.

In a few months' time, I would approach Oprah again, but this time doing what Diane Hudson feared most— writing about the TV queen for the tabloids.

7

ADDICTED TO ADDICTIONS

AA, AIDS, and Ray
Los Angeles, California
July 1993

T he news that actor Ray Sharkey had AIDS hit me like a twenty-pound brick. The additional news that he had given the virus to two women was incomprehensible. My source told me he knew both women personally. They were devastated, not only because they had the disease, but also because Ray had assured each of them that he was HIV-negative.

The news stunned me because only a few years back, I had seen Ray with his now ex-wife, Carole Graham, and their baby daughter at an Alcoholics Anonymous (AA) meeting, where Ray was accepting a cake to celebrate his many years of sobriety. Ray had stood in front of more than two hundred people and expressed how grateful he was to be clean and sober and that he couldn't have done it without AA. He told stories about how he would use heroin and cocaine on the set of his films. He would have it delivered to his trailer, get loaded, and then attempt to deliver a passable performance. It had taken him seven years, four drug-related car accidents, and several overdoses to finally realize that he had a serious problem.

The two women whom Ray passed AIDS to were both in recovery and had met Ray through AA. My source told me that Ray's T-cell count was 350. A normal count is 800, so Ray wasn't doing very well. One of the infected women was a twenty-five-year-old actress by the name of Elena Monica. On April 29, 1991, Elena had met Ray at an AA meeting in West Hollywood. He was separated from Carol at the time and was dating many women. Elena was instantly taken by Ray's animal magnetism and biker-boy looks. They began seeing each other incessantly and slept together soon after. The first question out of Elena's mouth before they went to bed was, "Did you ever take an AIDS test?"

"Of course," Ray replied. "In fact, I've been tested three times in the past year and a half, and the results have always come up negative. But I'll take another test if it will ease your mind."

"Yes," said Elena. "It would."

Ray supposedly took another test and told her the results were negative. For some reason, she didn't ask to see the results. My source told me that the other woman, Gail, was in bad shape but wasn't talking to the press.

After getting off the phone with my source, I ran into Bob's office and told him about the story. I knew we couldn't print anything about Sharkey or Monica having AIDS unless they first admitted it because the story contained all the ingredients for an instant lawsuit. I needed some proof.

That night I tried to contact Herb Nanas, Ray's manager, but he was perpetually out to lunch. I tried to contact Elena, but she, too, never answered her phone. I chose not to leave a message on her machine because I felt the mere fact that I was a tabloid reporter might scare her away. I decided to wait until morning to pursue other avenues.

The next day, Bob came into the office looking chipper as ever. He slammed a bunch of legal papers on my desk. "Read," he commanded. The papers were from a Los Angeles court and they named Elena Monica and Ray Sharkey. Elena was suing Ray for "intentionally transmitting" the AIDS virus.

Go girl.

I was thrilled. Not only was she willing to stand up for herself, but she was courageous enough to go public with her disease. Not many women want the world to know they have AIDS. Elena chose to tell her story, to try and obtain justice, to make a difference in the way women view sex and trust.

In the court papers, Elena made a startling allegation. She claimed that from July to October of 1991—for three months after she found out she had contracted the AIDS virus—Ray continued to have unprotected sex with her. Elena had told him she had AIDS, but she didn't yet know from whom she had contracted it. According to Monica's lawyer, Howard Harris, Ray had said to Elena, "God doesn't want me to get AIDS, so I have nothing to worry about." Elena believed him and they continued to have sex.

I went on a mission to find Elena and talk with her. Bob gave me a couple of addresses. One was her sister's house in Beverly Hills, and the other was Elena's apartment. I tried her sister's house first and had no luck. I went to Elena's apartment and rang the doorbell several times, but no one answered. I figured that word of the lawsuit had gotten out, and the media vermin were burning up her phone lines. I decided to wait in my car for a couple of hours just in case.

I looked her up in the *Players' Directory,* a book containing pictures of actors and their agents' phone numbers. She was absolutely beautiful, with long chestnut hair and big brown eyes. As I stared at her photo, I couldn't help but think that this girl would probably be dead in a couple of years. How was she handling the fact that she had basically been given a death sentence? What was her family's reaction? I wanted to talk with her to find out, so I waited.

She never showed.

I decided to leave a note stating where I was from and what I wanted to discuss with her. As I started to write, a lot of unexpected thoughts and feelings came out. I told her I was a member of Overeaters Anonymous and wanted to support her in what she was going through. I wrote two pages and left the note taped to her door. Even though most reporters wouldn't think of baring their souls in the midst of working on a story, I felt the need to separate myself from being a reporter, and for once approach the story as a human being.

To my surprise, I received a phone call from Elena the next day. She told me I was the only reporter she had contacted personally, and even though she wasn't giving any interviews, she wanted to thank me for the note. When I asked how she was doing, Elena simply stated, "I trust God and know that He is taking care of me. I know that everything happens for a reason, and I am learning to deal with this disease one day at a time. I don't hate Ray, I just feel sorry for him. Sorry that he could commit such a heartless act, sorry that he had to hurt so many women, sorry that he lied to me through it all. But I'm not going to spend however many days I have left on this earth feeling angry. I'm going to spend them healing, praying to God, and living my life to the fullest."

"Why did you decide to call me?" I asked.

"It was your note. I loved the things you said in your note, and since you're also a member of OA, I felt I could trust you."

"Thanks. I meant every word."

I was truly touched by my conversation with Elena, enough to want to quit the tabloid business and go into therapy. I thanked her for calling me and added that I was available to talk with her, off the record, anytime she wanted.

I wrote the story that afternoon, and it made the cover of the *Star.* But that wasn't the end of the Sharkey saga.

On July 29, 1992, Ray was arrested for possession of narcotics—presumably heroin—in Vancouver, British Columbia. Ray was there filming a new television series called "The Hat Squad" and had reportedly received a package from Los Angeles that contained the drug. When customs officials inspected the parcel at the airport, they found the heroin and immediately turned it over to the narcotics squad, who in turn went to Sharkey's hotel room with a search warrant. In the room they found more heroin and cocaine. Sharkey was arrested but released on a promise to appear in court.

In five words, Sharkey's life was a mess. But that still wasn't the end. The worst part came a few months later when Ray was hospitalized for pneumonia at Century City Medical Center in Los Angeles. Bob told me to go to the hospital to see if he was, in fact, checked in. I knew that hospital stakeouts were extremely difficult and nasty due to high security, but I trudged on anyhow. I went to the fourth-floor Special Care Unit, which handles people with AIDS and other contagious diseases, and nonchalantly walked around looking for Sharkey's room. I saw sights that made my stomach drop and my eyes water. People were hooked up to machines, looking like they were on their last leg of life. I finally stumbled upon a room that had a large sign on the door: "Do not enter, under any circumstances, without first checking with the nurse's station." I sneaked in. I knew I could have been caught and booted out, but at that moment I didn't care. I just wanted to get the story.

I took a deep breath and walked in the room. I almost keeled over when I saw what Sharkey looked like. He was thin as a skeleton and pale as a ghost. A picture of the old Ray shot through my mind: tan skin, muscular body, quite a hunk. But now he could hardly turn his head to see who was entering the room. He asked me who I was, and I softly told him that I was from *Star* magazine and I wanted to have a few words with him. He looked me up and down and asked me to have a seat.

The moment I sat down, his phone rang and he turned to see where it was. He achingly looked down at the floor where the ringing phone lay and slowly tried to turn his body to pick it up. I asked him if he needed help and he nodded, so I walked around the bed and picked up the phone for him. As he spoke with the person on the other end, his voice never raised to more than a whisper. He said he didn't want any visitors.

Ray finally hung up the phone, turned to me, and asked, "Who are you?"

"I'm a reporter from *Star* magazine," I repeated. "I just want to know how you're holding up and if you have any words for our readers."

"You can see how I'm holding up. Tell your readers to pray for me, that's all I ask. Thank them for their support. You know, I'm not supposed to have any visitors. You seem like a nice girl, and I don't want to get you into trouble, but could you please leave? It's hard for me to talk."

I nodded, thanked him for his time, and left. I exited the hospital in dismay. I felt overwhelmed by our meeting but had to get back into reporter mode and write the story.

The next day, *Star* sent David and a paparazzo, Rochelle Law, to get a photo of Ray lying on his deathbed. They found the room, and while David acted as a decoy, frantically asking the nurses where the nearest florist was, Rochelle took the shots. By the time Ray tried to call a nurse, David and Rochelle were gone. The photo, along with my story, made a two-page spread in the *Star* that week, and millions of readers were able to see the slow death of a movie star.

The issue sold over four million copies.

Two months later, Sharkey was dead.

Paying the Price of Tabloid Reporting
Los Angeles, California
September 1992

When actress Catherine Oxenberg of TV's "Dynasty" entered the Sierra-Tucson Center for Eating Disorders and
Addictions to get treatment for bulimia, I thought the story
would be a breeze to cover. I had met Oxenberg years ago
at an Overeaters Anonymous meeting and knew a lot about
her past. Even though it was against OA policy to break the
anonymity of its members, I knew Oxenberg's bulimia had
already been revealed in the *Globe,* so I didn't think writing
an article for the *Star* would be considered taboo.

Boy, was I wrong. To my dismay, the assignment ended
up being one of the most nightmarish of my career. In a
two-week period, I lost one longtime friend, got cursed at
on the phone, and had to chase down a mail carrier to retrieve what could have been incriminating evidence.

I spoke to a friend of mine who also knew Oxenberg
well. She confirmed that Catherine was recovering from
bulimia and anorexia at the $850-a-day facility in sunny Ar-
izona and that her disorder included severe usage of diet
pills, starvation, and binging and purging.

Three days after I began to gather the information, Bob
got a call from a woman named J.C., who swore she had
tons of dirt on Oxenberg and was willing to sell it to the
Star for the bargain price of $5,000. For some reason, Bob
took a liking to the woman and told her that reporter Steve
Tinney and I would meet her to discuss the details and
would bring along $5,000 in cash.

The woman threw a fit.

"I don't want to meet Lysa and Steve," she whined.
"Lysa knows who I am and will give away my identity. I
want to meet you and only you."

Bob assured her that I wouldn't give away her identity;
that I was there only to get the details and that was it.

She wouldn't buy it.

Steve and I tiptoed into Bob's office to listen in. "Okay, okay, I'll meet you on the corner of Wilshire and Barrington in one hour. A white car. Yeah, I got it. Cheers." *Click.*

Bob looked at us as though he was about to be taken to the guillotine. "She wants me to meet her on a street corner in an hour," he growled. "She told me to park my car, then she'd pick me up and take me to her apartment."

"Sounds fishy," I said. "Are you sure she's not a call girl?"

"I don't know. New York wants the stuff. They okayed the five grand. If you ask me, she sounds like a nut case I'd rather not deal with, but business is business."

He returned one hour later, handed me two pages of typed notes about Oxenberg, and told me to incorporate them into my story. J.C.'s information was brutal indeed. She said that Catherine had thrown up and taken diet pills for years, that she was totally obsessed with her body, and that her career was going downhill fast. My story emerged as a dark and depressing account of Oxenberg's eating disorder.

Two days later, Bob told me to rewrite my story without J.C.'s information. He wouldn't give me a reason.

When the story came out, I was stunned to see the headline (headlines are written by copy editors, not reporters): CATHERINE OXENBERG ADMITS TO POPPING DIET PILLS AND LAXATIVES—EVEN WHILE PREGNANT.

I knew the article would get a lot of flak, and sure enough, the next day Oxenberg's publicist called and said she was going to take legal action if a retraction wasn't published.

The same day, my longtime friend Michelle informed me that Catherine had shown up at a Monday night OA meeting and had gone up to the podium to announce, "Lysa Moskowitz wrote an article about how I was in an eating disorder clinic, and she revealed intimate details regarding my battle with bulimia. I think she should be banned from OA meetings."

Since I hadn't attended a meeting in years, the prospect of being banned didn't bother me. What bothered me was that I was being blamed for the changes the editors made in my story. Once I completed a piece, I had no control over what revisions the New York editors would make. Michelle went on to tell me that she, too, was disgusted with the article and didn't think we could continue being friends as long as I worked for the *Star.* Our friendship ended right there on the phone.

I decided to call Catherine and tell her I was sorry. The minute I told her my name, she went crazy. She yelled, screamed, ranted, and raved about what an awful person I was. She told me she couldn't believe I had anything to do with a story about someone in OA.

"You're a fucking asshole," Catherine spat, "a fucking unbelievable asshole. I can't believe you had the nerve to write such lies. I will never forgive you for this, and if I ever see you at an OA meeting again, may God help you."

I tried to calm her by saying that the story they printed wasn't the one I had written. I told her that once I sent a story to the New York office, it was out of my hands, that the editors had the power to change my words and make them more sensational.

"You really hurt me," she continued. "I no longer have trust in OA meetings. I can no longer go there and spill my guts to all of those people. And I want you to know that it's because of you. You fucked up my life. You've made it nearly impossible for me to trust people again."

I knew that nothing I said was going to make her forgive me. I hung up the phone. I went home, unable to shake the sickly feeling I had inside. I felt like I needed to DO something to make things right, so I sat down and wrote Catherine a letter. I basically poured out my heart without restraint and quickly put the letter in the mailbox before I could change my mind.

An hour later, I told David what I had done, thinking he'd be proud of me. Instead, he insisted in no uncertain terms that I had to get the letter back because it could be used against me in a court of law. He said that by saying I was sorry, I was admitting I did something wrong, and therefore I was admitting guilt. He told me to never, ever put apologies in print.

Great.

I went to the post office and asked what time the mail would be picked up from our building's box. The woman told me it was somewhere between 12:00 and 12:30, so I went to the box at 11:45 and waited for the mail carrier to show up. When he did, I explained that I had mailed a letter to the wrong address, and I desperately needed to get it back. He looked through the box and found my letter but said it was illegal for him to give it back to me because I was not the addressee. I'd have to go to the main post office in Beverly Hills and retrieve it later that afternoon. I went to the post office, retrieved the letter, and promptly ripped it to shreds.

Paula Goes Public
Los Angeles, California
June 1995

Paula Abdul didn't go public with her eating disorder until the end of 1995, when the folks at *People* magazine told her that if she didn't 'fess up to her disease, they would. I learned this directly from Paula in a conversation that should have been a tabloid reporter's dream. Instead, it turned out to be a decision between doing what was right and doing what I usually did—make money.

I had written many stories about Paula before I actually met her during the summer of 1995. I covered her rapid rise from an L.A. Lakers cheerleader to a Grammy Award-winning pop star and her equally rapid marriage to and divorce from Emilio Estevez. I was in the *Star* office the day reporter Diane Mannino came rushing in, saying she had gone to Santa Monica courthouse to pick up some documents when who of all people, Paula and Emilio, walked in to get married. She stayed long enough to capture a few photos and get a story from the clerk. The rush of excitement over an unexpected cover story shot through the office. I got the same feeling I had when I was once sent to look for Julia Roberts at the gym and bumped into her when I walked in the door.

My introduction to Paula Abdul came as a total surprise. I had been working out daily at a gym in Sherman Oaks called Billy Blanks. One morning, as I was leaving, I spotted Paula talking to a gorgeous, dark-haired male. My heart began racing as money signs flashed in front of my eyes. I had read weeks earlier that Paula had been released from an eating disorder treatment center where she had been recovering from bulimia. No one had captured the pop star on film since her release, and I knew a photo of her in workout clothes would be worth at least $1,500 to the U.S. tabloids, not to mention overseas. The only problem was, I did not have a camera. Luckily, there was a photo store a few doors down and I raced to purchase a disposable camera.

I've always been chicken about bolting in front of someone's face and snapping a photo. Paparazzi are notorious for being rude and invasive and have no problem jamming their cameras in front of celebrities. I didn't want to make a scene since the owners of the gym knew me, so I decided to put on my best acting job and lie to get her attention.

As soon as she broke away from her conversation, I ran up to her and whispered, "Ms. Abdul, I'm a big fan of yours and I wanted to tell you my cousin is in the hospital for bulimia and I've been in OA for seven years. I read about your recovery and my cousin would be thrilled to have a photo of you. Would you mind if I shot one?"

"Of course not," said Paula. "In fact, let's take one together." With that, she handed the camera to a woman nearby and told her to shoot away. I knew that if I was in the photo, the value would go down enormously. Tabloids aren't interested in posed pictures of celebrities and their fans. They like spontaneous, candid stuff: shots in which the star is unaware her or his picture is being taken. It was too late for me to be sneaky, so I posed with Paula. After the shots were taken, she hugged me and asked if I wanted to chat. I said sure. I was totally unprepared for what came next.

We sat down in a corner and she began to spill her guts.

"Getting abstinent is one of the hardest things I've ever done. Every day I want to binge and throw up and every day I have to remind myself that it's not an option," said Paula. "Was it that way for you at the beginning?"

"At the first OA meeting I attended, I made a decision to stop bulimia for good," I answered. "I didn't care what it took, I only knew I wouldn't achieve anything if I continued on a self-destructive path."

"I think it was difficult for me to realize how serious my bulimia had become, because everything on the outside was going so well," continued Paula. "You know, when I was at the height of my success with the song 'Straight Up,' my bulimia was at its worst. This should have been the happiest time of my life, but I didn't know how to deal with all the attention I was getting. I also began having problems with my sister, who was sick of being referred to as 'Paula Abdul's sister.' There was a lot of jealousy on her part and I felt guilty for having it all while she struggled in life. I guess the only way for me to show her how guilty I felt was to self-destruct."

We laughed. I was amazed by her openness. Then she showed me her hands. "Look at the scars I have from shoving my fingers down my throat," said Paula. "I would push and push until the food came up. I was so persistent in my attempts to purge myself of every morsel, that I would shove my fingers as far down as I could. I was the type of bulimic who binged on at least 10,000 calories at a time. It wasn't unusual for me to finish off an entire cake and bag of chocolate chip cookies in addition to a gallon of cookie dough ice cream and three cans of Diet Coke, all in one sitting. At least my teeth aren't eroded and my heart is okay."

"When did you start having problems?" I asked.

"I used to be chunky. Everyone in high school teased me about my baby fat and my big, bumpy nose. I got my nose fixed a few years later, but the baby fat was impossible to lose. I tried everything: diet pills, diuretics, laxatives, exercise, sex. Nothing worked. A friend of mine told me how she could eat whatever she pleased and not gain a pound. When she first spoke of throwing up, I thought it was the most disgusting, wretched act I had ever heard. A few years later, I became a Laker girl and was faced with a team full of gorgeous cheerleaders who had perfect physiques. I struggled to lose the extra weight. One day, when I was feeling depressed, I binged on potato chips and cookies. I was so sick to my stomach I didn't think I'd need to stick my finger down my throat to make the food come up. I drank a large glass of warm water like my friend had told me to do and I leaned over the toilet, pressed my hand to my stomach, and *voilà,* the food began to emerge. I threw up about three times before I felt exhausted but relieved. My eyes were extremely puffy afterward and there were tiny red dots around them. I never thought it was the beginning of my descent into the throes of an eating disorder, but I guess you never think it will become an addiction."

Encouraged by her candidness, I told her about my own struggle with bulimia and that I was writing a book about my experiences. Paula said she'd like to read it. Then, out of nowhere, she began talking about the tabloids.

"The hardest thing when I got out of the hospital was fending off tabloid reporters and paparazzi," she confided. When she said the words *tabloid reporters,* I froze up. I went from feeling like a good friend to a sleazebag.

She went on. "Photographers would camp outside my house, waiting like hungry wolves for me to emerge so they could take a bite. I had to hide my face behind a baseball cap whenever I went out. I even had to stop having OA meetings at my house because of the snitches at the meetings who would sell my story to the papers. It broke my heart when I read quotations of what I had revealed at an OA meeting in *Star* magazine."

I looked around to see if there were any rocks I could crawl under. I forced myself to keep talking. "It's hard to trust people, especially when you're rich and famous. You never know someone's motive when you meet them, and you always have to be on guard," I said. "Now that you're single, dating must be difficult."

"It is," admitted Paula. "I knew it wasn't going to work out between Emilio and me when we got married. Minutes before I said 'I do,' a voice inside told me to run. Don't get me wrong, Emilio is a great guy, but I really wasn't ready to tie the knot. He chased me for years and finally I was so tired of being alone that I agreed to go out with him. After our first date, he phoned me every day and pursued me with flowers, little gifts, and surprise dinners. He treated me better than any man ever had. I loved him more like a friend than a husband. I desperately want to date a man who's not in the entertainment business, but it's difficult to find someone I can trust. I still hang out with the same women I hung with in high school, and I rarely reveal myself to strangers. I don't know why I'm opening up to you since I don't know you, but you're a recovering bulimic and I feel we have a silent bond. You're also very easy to be with."

I sat there feeling good that I had been there to listen to Paula in an unjudgmental way, but I also felt like a liar and a snake. This was something I struggled with often. On the one hand, I needed to make money to support myself, and on the other hand, the way I made money was at the expense of other people. I knew the facts I revealed often caused embarrassment and hurt, especially when I revealed a star's innermost secrets.

Paula suddenly stood up. "I have to go now, but I would love to hang out with you again. Maybe we could have coffee after a workout or go see a movie."

"I'd love to," I answered. She asked me for my phone number, and I promptly wrote it down. I didn't ask for hers because I knew stars were cautious about giving out their home numbers. We hugged good-bye and said we'd meet again later in the week.

I left knowing I had a $2,000 story on my hands, but I decided not to sell it. After that day, I stopped working out at Billy Blanks and changed my phone number. I'd still like to send Paula a copy of my book on bulimia, but I doubt she'll want to read it after she reads this.

Who Cares About Friends? I Need Cash
Los Angeles, California
December 1995

Fans of sexy "Married . . . With Children" star Christina Applegate were shocked to learn she had traded in her blond bimbo image and was seeking God by joining a trendy Los Angeles church called Agape. The twenty-four-year-old actress had been attending services at the church every Wednesday night and Sunday morning for over a year and was enrolled in its Science of Mind class.

I stumbled on Applegate when I myself was enrolled in the Science of Mind course. The leader was taking attendance and called out the name Applegate. A thin girl with blunt orange hair, large black-rimmed glasses, and a polka-dot granny dress stood up and said "Here." I was stunned to see the transformation Christina had made from eye-popping California blonde to thrift-shop matron. In my head, the words *cover story* reverberated, but as with Paula Abdul, I was left with a moral struggle. Was it right to sell my story while taking a spiritual class? It was like having sex in church. It's dirty and sneaky, but thrilling to get away with.

I was low on money at the time and decided to put aside my spiritual values long enough to sell the story to the *Star.* Once I began scouting the church for potential sources, I was surprised to find how many of Christina's "close" friends would talk. One girl—I'll call her Nancy—was more than happy to spill the beans about Christina once I told her she could make $500 for the information. We got into my car minutes after she hugged Christina good-bye after a Sunday church service. We drove to a nearby coffeehouse, where Nancy proceeded to dish the dirt.

"The only reason I'm doing this is because I'm out of acting work right now and I need the cash," explained Nancy. "I usually would never think of selling out my friends, but when the rent is due, it becomes a choice between survival and integrity. I've usually chosen survival."

I assured her I would keep her name confidential and do nothing to reveal the fact that she had sold out Christina.

"I met her at Agape one Sunday," continued Nancy. "I didn't recognize her at first. I just started dancing and singing to the choir with her, and we began chatting when the service was over. She introduced herself as 'Christ'ina, putting an emphasis on the *Christ.* Every Sunday afterward we would say hello, but it wasn't until I enrolled in the Science of Mind course and was assigned to the same group as her that we really started to get close. I asked her how she got involved in Agape and she told me she wasn't happy with the way her life was going. Before Agape, she was staying out all night at clubs like the Viper Room and Roxbury, drinking and partying. After her pal River Phoenix died, Christina contemplated her life and decided to make a radical change and devote her existence to helping others by finding God. A friend told her about Agape, which is different from other nondenominational churches. The moment Christina stepped into the church sanctuary, she said she felt a change come over her. A week later, she dyed her bleached-blond hair red, cut it off to a short bob, and replaced her sexy clothing with thrift-shop jeans, sweaters, and nerdy glasses. She immediately enrolled in the fifteen-week Science of Mind Tuesday night class to further her studies and spiritual practice."

Science of Mind is an intensive course that teaches the principle that there is One Universal Reality, One God, One Ultimate Being, and we are all connected to that source of light and power. It is not a cult. It does not teach its members to worship a person. It teaches people to find their own source of power and simply "be here for God." I learned Christina was taking the class so she could go on to become a licensed Agape practitioner. She is apparently very serious about changing her beliefs and about helping others through her acting. For a long time she had felt ashamed by the image she was portraying as Kelly Bundy. In the future, she wants to take more responsibility and put more thought into the roles she accepts.

"I didn't even recognize Christina. Someone had to point her out to me," another source told me. "She looked and acted nothing like Kelly Bundy. She talks about finding a deep peace within her soul. When she comes into the church, she leaves her image and ego at the door."

I went home and felt good about writing a story with a positive, uplifting message. Christina has made it clear that she no longer wants to be associated with the blond bimbo image. Even though she still appears on "Married . . . With Children," she has learned to separate herself from her role as Kelly Bundy and bring God to the set each day.

After her contract ends on "Married," Christina wants to devote her life to making quality films and helping others find themselves. I'm glad I got to play a part in relaying her message.

8

IN THE TRENCHES

Tatum's Boytoy and John's Sweet Young Thing
Los Angeles and Malibu, California
December 1992

Just before I quit working exclusively for the *Star* in 1992, I was assigned to do a story about Tatum O'Neal's new boyfriend. Because she hadn't been spotted with anyone since her ugly divorce from tennis brat John McEnroe, this was a big story in the eyes of *Star*'s editors. Bob gave me the boyfriend's address and the make and model of his car, as we had no idea what the guy looked like. Photographer Jim Knowles and I went to the address and were on constant lookout for a white Jeep. When one finally pulled up, thc driver looked more like an ex-con than a boytoy of Tatum's. He sported a fashionable buzz cut, round specs, and a grungy T-shirt. Nirvana blasted from his speakers and his pet Doberman panted heavily out the window.

Jim tried to take a picture of the guy, but missed as the

Jeep entered the gated parking lot. I phoned his apartment from the outside monitor and told him who I was and why I was there. I politely asked him if he was dating Tatum O'Neal and he shouted a loud "NO" through the speaker.

Jim and I decided to wait around, just in case the guy came out again. To our surprise, he drove out of the garage a half hour later, blasting Guns N' Roses. Stupidly, Jim dashed in front of the Jeep and snapped away with his camera. The boytoy leaped out, sprinted toward Jim, and tried to wrestle his camera away. Jim managed to kick the guy in the leg and take off. I watched all the action from my idling car less than a block away. As Jim drove off, I saw the Jeep follow him, and that's when I decided it was a good time to go for a burger and wait for Jim to call me from his hospital bed.

Jim phoned an hour later and said he had lost the guy on Wilshire Boulevard. I breathed a sigh of relief and called the office. One of the reporters told me that the guy had just called and threatened to rough me up if I printed anything about his nonexistent affair with Tatum O'Neal. He firmly added that he wouldn't hesitate to severely hurt Jim if he ever came near his apartment again.

From that experience, I learned never to reveal my real name until I knew who I was dealing with. I've heard horror stories of reporters being threatened with guns and harassed by sources and celebrities.

A few months after the incident, the *Enquirer* assigned me to do a story on John McEnroe. I first had to find out which house in the Malibu Colony belonged to McEnroe and what pretty young thing he was living with. Since the entrance to the colony is blocked by a guard booth, it was my job to sneak onto the property via the beach.

I met up with a photographer, and we snuck onto the beach and walked hand in hand as if we were lovers. My source had described, in lame details, what McEnroe's house looked like. He told me it had a forest green roof. I had counted five already. He also said that it had a large patio with a pool, and large glass windows. Every house had one. Should I stop now?

We were stumped. I noticed a few construction workers, and I decided to try to con my way through the backyard of one of the mansions.

"Excuse me," I said in a sweet, virginal voice. "My friend is having a party in one of these houses, and I wanted to surprise her. Can I cut through your backyard and get to the house from the street?"

"But of course," said one of the workers. I cut through and began jogging down the street in search of McEnroe's house. My source had also told me that there was brick in the front of John's house, and sure enough, the third to last house had huge stacks of bricks in front, large stained-glass windows, and an ugly green roof. There didn't seem to be anyone home, and I was afraid to hang around since I was on private property and could easily get arrested. I ran back to the beach and told the photographer that no one was home.

Just as we were about to pull away in his car, the photographer didn't notice a large pile of sandbags stacked in front of his car. He stepped on the gas before I could warn him and drove right on top of the bags. For the next two hours, we ended up having to shovel the car out of the sand, then refill the bags with new sand from the beach.

As the photographer was finishing up, I took his binoculars and looked through the gate into McEnroe's driveway. A black Mercedes was parked there. I quickly took down the license plate number and ran it through the DMV.

I later found out that the woman who owned the Mercedes was a happily married socialite who was simply taking care of John's house while he was away. I also found out that the entire lead was a lie. But I decided to keep that information from the editors at the *Enquirer*, since they had just spent $150 for me to check out the house and $250 for the photographer.

Elvis Reborn
Los Angeles, California
April 1989

My introduction to the hell of never-ending stakeouts came only a month after I started working at the Star, *when we were convinced that the delivery of Lisa Marie Presley's child was imminent. More than six weeks later, through innumerable car chases, a twenty-four-hour rotating watch on three houses, and a near fatality, she had the kid and we missed it completely.*

The fun started when reporter Alvin Grimes and I were called into Barry Levine's office and made to sign papers swearing we wouldn't reveal Lisa Marie's address to the competition, because the Enquirer *was offering more than $10,000 just for a street number. Why such a big deal? Well, this was at the height of the "I spotted Elvis at the Tastee-Freez in Biloxi" craze, and this was the King's first grandchild. Steve LeGrice, the hard-charging news editor, referred to it as the biggest tabloid story of the last ten years. It was to be a real head-to-head contest between the tabs to see who could get the juiciest details and the most embarrassing candid shots of the very pregnant Lisa Marie waddling through supermarket parking lots. At the* Star, *we couldn't always compete with the superior funding and manpower of the* Enquirer, *so we had to pick our battles. This was to be one of them.*

The paranoia was total. Barry marked the location for us in a Thomas Guide; then, realizing in horror that spies in the office could find out where the house was, he ripped the page out and stuffed it into his desk drawer. In turn, he realized that a map book with one page missing was a dead giveaway as to which neighborhood the house was in, so he promptly stuffed the whole book into his desk.

"You can't be too careful," he cautioned, eyes darting around. "Trust no one. Tell nobody where this is, or you

will be summarily fired, and the Star will start legal proceedings against you for breach of confidentiality."

Alvin started needling him. "What if we talk in our sleep and our girlfriends hear and sell it to the Enquirer?"

"Don't sleep with your girlfriends! That's an order!" Barry barked. "Do you talk in your sleep?"

"How am I supposed to know? I'm sleeping. What if they bug our bedrooms?"

"Sleep on the couch!"

"What if we go out for a beer after work and an Enquirer reporter is there and starts buying us drinks and we get really drunk and accidentally spill the beans?"

"You are not to drink with any strange people. Besides, you know that Enquirer reporters look like giant rats."

Alvin was clearly enjoying himself. "But what if we're drinking with someone else, and we get drunk and talk to them while an Enquirer reporter is there and overhears?"

"Alvin, you are not to talk to anyone strange in the bar!"

"But what if I want to pick up women?"

"What about your girlfriend?"

"You just said I couldn't sleep with her."

"Get out! Get out of my office! You're giving me a headache."

We went into Robert's office, where he had piles of cellular phones, walkie-talkies, and antennas. We got vouchers to rent whatever cars we wanted at Avis. Barry suspected ubiquitous sleaze paparazzo Phil Ramey had a modified police scanner that could pick up cell phone conversations, and he insisted we all talk in bizarre bad-spy-movie code whenever we called. I was Mr. Purple. Alvin was Mr. White. Lisa Marie was the Pouty Princess. Priscilla Presley's mansion was Gramma's House.

I'll admit it: There was a certain James Bondian thrill about it all. Car chases, secret code words, stakeouts, hiding from the cops, electronic eavesdropping, aerial reconnaissance, unseen nefarious enemies . . . it was all very

cloak-and-dagger. Fun, even, in a childish way. Until things
started to get out of hand.

On the second day of the stakeout, I showed up at 6 A.M.
to relieve Alvin, unfolded a sunshade in the front windshield, hung dry cleaning in the side windows, and
crouched in the backseat, peering over the trunk, waiting
for one of the Presleys' cars to come out of the gate. A car
came screeching up behind me. My heart leaped. A competitor? Come to drag me away for ruthless interrogation
in the dungeons below the Enquirer newsroom in Lantana,
Florida? Security guards hired to beat me to a pulp?
Twitchy neighborhood-watch people with a sawed-off 12-
gauge and a head full of coke?

No, it was Rochelle Law, one of the few woman paparazzo in a very macho business. She was thin, dark-haired,
and bore a striking resemblance to Popeye's girlfriend
Olive Oyl. It was she who had sold us the address, and she
who had been staking it out eighteen hours a day by herself
for three weeks before we arrived. I could tell she had been
in a car by herself just a little too long. She babbled nonstop
the entire time we were together. I got the feeling I was the
first human she had spoken to in weeks.

For about a week, the Star team had the location to ourselves, and we were careful to park blocks away from the
Presleys and follow them from a long distance. But all good
things come to an end, and one fine afternoon, Phil Ramey
showed up, grinning like the Cheshire Cat, with two flunk-
ies and a TV crew in tow. They parked right in front of the
house, conspicuously unloading their gear, and got into
an immediate confrontation with Lisa Marie's husband,
Danny Keough. Garbage cans were flung. We left as the
police cars were pulling up.

The situation deteriorated rapidly. Not long afterward,
Priscilla's race-car driver husband, Marco Garibaldi, tried
to ram reporter Donna Balancia's car in Beverly Hills and
pursued Donna in his Jeep, swerving aside only at the last
moment. I followed Priscilla and Marco from Lisa Marie's

house right up to the entrance of the road they lived on in Beverly Hills. I gave them five minutes to park and start unloading their car. Then I drove up, parked my car, walked to the gate, and peeked through the cracks, trying to see if they were (as rumored) unloading medical equipment so Lisa could have the baby at home, frustratingly safe from our prying eyes.

BEEEEEEEEEP! I whirled around and my worst nightmare came true. Busted. Priscilla and Marco had evidently taken a back route in and arrived after I did, only to find me bent over and looking through their gate. The Jeep followed about an inch from my ankles as I trudged back up the hill to my car, red-faced.

The situation was losing its humor.

I was making friends with the Presleys' neighbors, who by now knew who each of us was and what we were doing there. They even helped now and again, telling us we had missed Priscilla leaving while we were chasing Danny, or offering to break in and induce labor to put an end to the stakeout.

The weeks had dragged on and on, and by now it seemed obvious we had miscalculated the amount of time she was pregnant. It seemed no human could take the pain of ten months of pregnancy for more than a few days. We bagged the stakeout for a weekend and checked into the Sunset Marquis and Chateau Marmont to get pictures of Roseanne Barr as she reunited with the daughter she had given up for adoption years before.

On Memorial Day, we lounged by the pool, the Roseanne story successfully wrapped, ready to switch gears back to Lisa Marie. Barry had given us the day off (thanks, it was a holiday anyway) and told us to be ready to go back to work on Tuesday.

That night I got an urgent call. Lisa Marie had gone to St. John's Hospital in Santa Monica and had the baby. We had missed the story after spending months and tens of thousands of dollars.

The fat was in the fire.

I immediately went to St. John's and talked a parking lot attendant into showing me an entrance doctors used to get into the hospital. I was wearing cowboy boots and my footsteps resounded like gunshots in the darkened, deserted corridors. On my shoulder was a small black duffel bag. In the bag was a small automatic camera. I had been told the first picture of the baby was worth over $200,000. That estimate turned out to be off by at least $300,000.

At any rate, I knew that with one picture I could kiss this entire headache good-bye. The source said she was on the third floor. When I got there, the entire wing had been cleared out for Lisa Marie. It was as silent as a grave. I darted from darkened room to darkened room, pausing at each to catch my breath and listen for guards. My heart hammered so hard my whole torso shook. Finally, I was just around the corner from where her room was. I closed my eyes, firmed my resolve, and turned the corner . . .

. . . and four security guards posted in front of her door pivoted as one, their eyes locking onto me like targeting lasers. I almost passed out. They came over and started bumping into me, trying to see if I was carrying a concealed weapon. One of them felt the metallic bulk of the camera. They demanded to know who I was and what I was doing there.

Luckily a guardian angel nurse approached and said, "I'll help the poor man find who he's looking for." I stammered a name out of the air. Not surprisingly, it didn't show up in the computer.

I said thanks and headed for the exit.

Behind me I heard, "You there, freeze! I said halt!"

I took off running, reached the stairwell, and took the flights leaping, one ten-foot-drop at a time. They were following. I hit the parking garage and ran for my car. They were following, weaving between the pillars in the darkness, still on my tail. I screeched out of the garage without paying, tires smoking, heart pounding, head spinning. I picked up the cell phone and dialed the office. "Barry, I just got caught at the hospital. Four security guards chased me all the way to the garage."

I looked in the rear-view mirror. They were following. In a big Chevy, weaving across lanes. "Barry! They're still behind me! What should I do?"

"Lose 'em and call me back," he said and hung up. Lose them. Why, I would have never thought of that on my own.

I did manage to lose them, although for legal reasons I can't really reveal how.

The next day, the whole office was prepped for an all-out assault on the St. John's maternity ward. We were to come back with the picture of the baby or not come back at all.

It was like the British charging into German machine-gun fire at the Somme in World War I. We didn't stand a chance.

An Enquirer *reporter was dressed as a priest. Jamie was in a patient's gown, a camera hidden in her underwear. Jennifer had a bouquet with a camera in it. Donna Balancia was dressed as a nurse. I was dressed in doctor's scrubs, a stethoscope around my neck and a clipboard under my arm. I got to the third floor, got off the elevator, and took three steps. Waiting at the nurses' station were the same guards from last night and four real cops. A guard looked at me. Then down at a sheet of paper.*

He pointed a thick finger. "You." He hooked a thumb back over his shoulder. "Out."

Eloquent in its minimalism. I didn't stay to argue.

A photo was eventually sold to the Star *by the Presleys themselves and a photographer who had once done them a favor. I was told that the* Star *and* People *magazine together paid about $500,000 for the right to have that baby on their covers that week. Worldwide, the photo is said to have brought in about $1 million. The photographer and the Presleys split it.*

We returned to the office bloodied and dejected. Barry was crestfallen. He was going to have to answer for our failure to be on top of the story, our failure to get the picture, and the outlandish expenditure of money, equipment, and manpower put into this fiasco. It would not be pleasant.

I wanted to console him. "Barry," I said, "I had the strangest dream about this whole situation last night. I dreamed we were at the hospital waiting and Lisa and Danny came down. And we just started talking. I made friends with Danny and we went to get his truck out of parking. When we came back, we were horrified. You had tied Lisa Marie up, stripped her naked, and were trying to stuff the baby back up her so you could take pictures of it being born."

Barry managed a feeble smile. "Dream, Dave? Didn't that really happen?"

Who Flew the Coop With the Maid?
Hollywood, California
May 1993

When Tony Frost from the *Enquirer* sent me on a wild goose chase after actor Richard Mulligan from the television show "Empty Nest," I had no idea why I was going to Mulligan's house or what I was after. All Tony told me was, "Go to a bookshop, buy Mulligan a book, have it wrapped, and deliver it to his house. Then call me."

I bought Richard a book on codependent relationships. When I arrived at his door, a short blond woman answered. I asked if Richard was home. "No," she snapped. I told her I had something to deliver personally and that I'd wait until he got home if it was okay with her.

It wasn't.

She grabbed the book out of my hand and muttered, "I'll make sure he gets it."

I called Tony and told him what had happened. "Great job. Great job," he raved.

"If delivering a book is considered doing a great job, I should be getting more money for assignments where I actually risk my life," I said.

"Spend the rest of the afternoon waiting outside Mulligan's house. Be sure and take note of whoever enters or leaves the premises."

A paparazzo arrived and we waited together in his ultra-modern pickup truck. After an hour of shooting the shit, I told him that it looked suspicious for us to be sitting in his truck across the street from Mulligan's place, so we drove around the block a few times. On our fifth trip around, I noticed a Hispanic woman walking down the street. She was about ten houses away from Richard's, but something inside me knew she would be entering his house.

She looked straight at me as she turned the corner. Then she walked right into Mulligan's house. The paparazzo was cursing at himself for not getting a shot of the woman. Five minutes later, the woman came out of the house and started down the street again. The paparazzo drove past her slowly and clicked away. The woman yelled in Spanish and gave the photographer the finger.

I still didn't know what I was after, so I called Tony and asked him what was up. Once again, he told me what a great job I was doing and that I needed to be back at the scene tomorrow; he would have more details for me then.

The next day, Tony told me I would be meeting a new paparazzo on the main strip of stores down the block from Richard's house. He told me to be very discreet when approaching the photographer because we were going to be following Mulligan's ex-wife, a porn star and stripper known as the "Anal Queen of Hollywood," who claimed Richard had been stalking her every day. She had told Tony that each day at noon, Richard would drive around until he found her, then get out of his car, corner her, and harass her.

Tony told me that the ex-wife would be coming out of a restaurant called Chan Dara around noon, and that we were to follow her and see if Richard showed up. If he did, the paparazzo was to get pictures as I tried to listen in on their conversation. I felt like an undercover cop doing a sting operation. James Bond music seemed to be playing in the background as I went about my day.

I spotted the paparazzo hiding behind a newspaper, staking out the restaurant from across the street. He looked anything but discreet, with his bushy hair, dark glasses, cellular phone, and oversize camera bag.

I expected Mulligan's ex-wife to look the part of a porn star, with bulging breasts and supple thighs. I pictured her wearing a skin-tight red dress, spiked heels, and no underwear. The woman who came out of the restaurant looked like an Ivory girl, sporting a demure sundress, dark glasses, and tan penny loafers. Her breasts were anything but bulging, and her legs were short and thin.

I'd heard through the grapevine that she was an extremely paranoid woman. David told me he had dealt with her before and that she was crazy. The paparazzo and I walked up and down the block for over two hours with no sign of Mulligan's car. The ex-wife finally decided to set up shop underneath a closed clothing boutique. She sat on a bench in front of the store and waited.

Finally, she signaled for me to come over. When I did, she whispered, "Richard had to go to a doctor's appointment, so he might not show up today. Just wait across the street for another hour."

"Sure," I mumbled. I went back to our station. "She's nuts," I told the paparazzo. "Completely nuts."

We sat in his car for another two hours. I called Tony and complained. He told me to wait until eight o'clock and then phone him back. I looked at my watch. It was only seven.

Finally, at eight o'clock, Mulligan's ex-wife got up and left the storefront. I called Tony and he said the assignment was finished for the night, but I would resume work the next morning. Another day of endless waiting was too much to bear, so I turned down the job.

A week later, the blazing headline that flashed on the front page of the *Enquirer* read, EMPTY NEST STAR RICHARD MULLIGAN IN BIZARRE RELATIONSHIP WITH HIS LIVE-IN MAID. The photo in the story showed the Hispanic woman I had seen entering Richard's house. Supposedly he had been having an affair with his housekeeper ever since his wife walked out. We had conned Mulligan's ex-wife into thinking we were interested in her story, when all the *Enquirer* really wanted was photos and information on the maid.

"Diff'rent Strokes" Kid Gone Bad
Las Vegas, Nevada
Winter 1991

It isn't often that tabloid journalists are actually allowed to interview celebrities. When we are, it is usually a bad sign. Either the celeb has fallen so far that ANY publicity, even in the scandal sheets, looks good, or the celeb is in such bad trouble that he or she needs to make a deal to put a favorable twist on his or her plight.

I once got to interview Dana Plato, one of the stars of the hit TV show "Diff'rent Strokes," in her jail cell after she robbed a video store armed with a pellet gun. Of course, I also paid her $25,000 of Star's money for the honor.

When we got a call from our Las Vegas stringer that Plato had been arrested, though the details were still sketchy, the story sounded too bizarre to be true. Only a year earlier, Plato had appeared nude in Playboy, looking fairly good but posing in suggestive, hard-core positions that seemed a little, well, tasteless for someone who was once on the highest-rated show on television.

I was immediately dispatched to Las Vegas with photographer Alan Zanger to find out what had really happened. We drove to a housing development in a suburb outside Las

Vegas, the kind of place where all the apartment buildings look the same, too perfect and orderly, like they've been stamped out of some giant yellow stucco Play-Doh factory. I went to the nearby strip mall and began trying to piece the case together.

Clerks in a dry-cleaning store where Plato had worked said that she had been out of work for months and was living with her boyfriend in a tiny apartment, scrounging for odd jobs, and sobbing to the customers in the bar next door about losing custody of her son. The barflies had already been bought up and told to keep silent by the Globe, *but I managed to collar a dirty, scruffy sixteen-year-old desert rat who said he had done "a lot of drugs with Dana until she got too fried out." The kid's eyes were tiny and wandering; obviously her absence hadn't inspired him to cut down.*

"Yeah, man, I like to get high, but I had to stop hanging around Dana."

"Why?"

"Well, she just got too extreme."

"Huh?"

"Well, she started shopliftin' Scotch-Gard from the 7-11 and inhaling that 'cause she said she couldn't get high off coke no more."

"You gotta be kidding."

"No, man, I swear. You pour it on a rag or something, put it in a baggie, and just huff and puff. Get higher than shit, bounce off the walls, giggle till you puke, all kinds of fun. Only problem is, it makes you dumb as a rock. For two days after I did it with her I couldn't even tie my own shoes. It brain-damages you. You'll see if you ever meet her."

"See what?"

"It's like she never came down. Always twitching and nervous, babbling real fast, can't remember shit, just a complete nut now."

I went to the convenience store, the video store she robbed, and the apartment complex she lived in and talked to the people who knew her. What emerged was a rather pathetic portrait of a child star whose time had passed, and who was desperately looking for a way to somehow fit into a society that didn't care about her anymore.

The day of the robbery she had been all over the neighborhood asking for work, even offering to pick up dogshit off the apartment complex lawn. Finally she went to the video store, wearing sunglasses and a ridiculous wig and toting a pellet gun, and demanded money. After she got a paltry sum, she ran out the back door, tossed off the wig, and got back to her apartment just in time to meet the cops. Poorly planned, absurdly executed, it was a senseless crime that made me feel unhinged just thinking about it.

I went to the Las Vegas jail, got the names and numbers of Plato's court-appointed lawyers, and phoned them in to Barry. The bidding war for an interview with Plato started almost immediately. Everyone wanted to know what was going through her head, what could have driven her to such a desperate strait. Her lawyers were two young guys just out of law school, much more accustomed to defending gang members and getting hookers out on bail. This was the most attention they'd ever received, and they were excited beyond words, determined to ride the case as far as they could.

Barry arrived at the Mirage Hotel and immediately checked into the biggest, most expensive suite they had. We were in direct competition with the Enquirer on the story. The lawyers were demanding cash in advance for the story to pay for Plato's bail.

Barry and I picked up a huge amount of cash via Western Union, cashed it, and walked through the casino with a briefcase full of what Barry said was in excess of $25,000. He turned to me halfway through and said, "You know, it's looking more and more like this is going to fall through. I'm tempted to throw all this down on red on the roulette wheel. We win, we're $25,000 richer and they'll never know the difference."

For a second the idea danced in my head. "Yeah, but imagine the explaining we'll have to do if we lose. We'd have to check out and head straight for the Mexican border. We'll be writing tourist brochures under assumed names in Cabo San Lucas." Barry laughed, but I knew I'd have to keep an eye on the briefcase if the situation turned sour.

Eventually, after a sit-down conference in the lawyers' pillbox of an office, where we drank tequila for three hours, the New York editor called and said, "I want the story. I don't care what it costs. Offer them the full $25,000."

It was a done deal. The lawyers warned us not to listen to anything Dana's boyfriend said because he just wanted the money. They feared as soon as he got his hands on any sum, he'd head for the hills. It was nice to have someone involved in the whole sordid mess to which I could feel morally superior.

I wondered where the line was in this case: We were technically enriching a felon far beyond what she could have ever hoped to gain from her actual crime. Right, wrong, illegal, legal, we didn't care. Would we be acting the same way if she were a horrible serial killer who tortured and killed helpless children? If she were a complete monster, would we still be helping her profit from her crimes so we could distill the story for our semiliterate audience?

Probably. And so would everyone else in the news business.

All we wanted was a picture of her in a prison uniform, acting like she was the victim of some great tragedy, along with a tearful account of her fall from fame and fortune.

We got it.

But as usual, it was not straightforward. The guards would not allow us to take a camera in when I did the initial interview. Plato's lawyers had to perjure themselves to a judge and claim that they needed pictures of Dana for some aspect of the defense. They were very eager to help us get the story, probably because our paying Plato was the only way they'd ever get their mitts on any real money in this case. I wondered what kind of a percentage they were demanding for setting up the deal.

Zanger wasn't allowed to take pictures of Plato until the day after I did the interview, and the photos ended up arriving in New York too late to make every edition, so most of the issues of the magazine had only a small shot of her looking pathetic on the cover. Zanger said she loved the attention; she cheered up when the camera lens was pointed at her. Must have seemed like old times. I saw the contact sheets of the shots. She was posing, pirouetting, acting sexy, hiking up her dress, pressing her breasts together to show her cleavage. I was eerily reminded of Norma Desmond in Sunset Boulevard.

On the day of the interview, I was searched by the guards, then locked into a bleak conference cell where lawyers meet with prisoners. I pulled out a tape recorder. Dana was brought in by a hefty prison matron. She was exactly like the drug-addict kid said. Her eyes darted everywhere. She jumped like a startled deer, trembled constantly, and talked in short, sharp rushes, barking with nervous laughter. If I hadn't known she was locked up by herself in "separate custody" (away from other tough women who would have beaten or raped her), I would have thought she was completely fried on coke. She was wearing a green dress. I remembered what reporter Donna Balancia had said, when she was in County Jail for unpaid parking tickets: "We were all in blue dresses, except for this one crazy chick who kept talking to herself. All the other girls said to stay away from the ones in the green dresses."

I wanted to start off the conversation on an easy note, get her talking about normal stuff before we got into the upsetting recent events.

No way.

We only had twenty minutes, and Barry wanted the blood and guts on the floor as soon as possible. So I asked her what it was like to be in jail, and she regressed to *talking like a four-year-old, saying it wasn't so bad, that she could see the trains go by and watch people walk the streets. She even got to feed a "cute widdle pigeon" some leftover bread crumbs. I asked her about using drugs and she began acting like a ninety-eight-year-old grandma: "Oh, goodness gracious, oh my heavens, no. Dear, dear. Gosh, I wouldn't do that."*

Behind her, I saw her lawyers roll their eyes and snort.

I asked her if she knew she could get ten years for her crime, and if she would be able to handle such a stiff sentence. "I don't know," she said in a tiny voice. She began to bite her nails. In the enclosed room, the crunching of her nails sounded like twigs breaking.

What would she do in jail to pass the time? "I don't know." Snap, snap, crack.

Our time was up, and the deputy who had been watching me through the wire-reinforced window, hoping I would pull out a camera so he could bust my head, ordered me out. As I stood to leave, Dana hugged me and said thanks.

I was about to write a scandal-filled story that would be reprinted around the world, revealing Dana's failure and degradation and driving the final stake into the heart of her career, and she was THANKING me?

She really had lost touch with reality, I decided.

Caught in the Act
Bel Air Estates, California
November 1993

It was the biggest shocker of the year, Ted Danson and Whoopi Goldberg shacked up at the ultra-expensive Hotel Bel Air—and David and I were lucky enough to catch them in the act.

A source of David's had tipped him off that Ted had been staying in room 364, a $1,000-a-night deluxe suite, since

November of 1992. The source was good pals with one of the hotel maids, and he was told that Whoopi had taken up semipermanent residence in the room as well. When I first heard the story, I thought it was totally absurd. Even an open-minded person like me couldn't see Ted Danson and Whoopi Goldberg in bed; but I, like the rest of the country, was shocked when I found out the story was true.

After David and I concocted a story about how we were celebrating our first wedding anniversary and wanted to get the same room as we had on our honeymoon, the front desk did some maneuvering and got us the room of our choice; one that just happened to be right behind Ted and Whoopi's. When we arrived at our $350-a-night, Santa Fe–style suite, complete with two TVs, a huge living room, stereo system, fireplace, kitchen, and bathtub/Jacuzzi, I felt like I'd died and gone to heaven.

We walked out of our room and discovered we could see right into Ted's. It amazed me that a celebrity as big as he was, who happened to be cheating on his wife, would choose a room in which people could see everything that was going on just by looking through the back window. The hotel had dozens of rooms located on higher floors, which would have provided total privacy, but Ted chose the accessible one.

The rumor going around Hollywood was that Ted's wife, Casey, had kicked him out of their million-dollar Pacific Palisades home when she found out he was fooling around with Whoopi. The news of her husband's infidelity shocked her so much that she ended up having a nervous breakdown and checked into a psychiatric hospital.

We met up with a photographer, and our first task was to find out if Whoopi was really there. Since we couldn't camp outside Ted's room, we had to take a subtler approach: We'd take turns nonchalantly strolling in the garden behind their room, and if one of us spotted the happy couple, he or she would cough or sneeze loudly to signal that it was clear to get a shot. After hours of staring at rare and exotic plants with no sign of Ted or Whoopi, we decided to check out the restaurant.

Since the Hotel Bel Air has infrared lights and cameras in all of the trees, the photographer had to keep his equipment hidden. Most photographers are experienced enough to know how to blend in, but some stick out like a sore thumb and end up ruining the assignment for everyone. We also had to stay on the lookout for rival reporters, who are the sneakiest creatures of all. We've had rival reporters do everything from calling security on us, to reporting us to the hotel manager, to calling our room posing as a source and tipping us off to the wrong information.

Right before dinner, David and I strolled by Danson's room. To our surprise, the shades were open and the lights were on, which meant someone had come home. We sat in the garden and chatted and waited and kissed and waited and kissed some more and waited and finally, as we got up to leave, I saw Whoopi in the flesh. David ran back to our room to phone the photographer, and I sneaked up to the window. I saw Ted walk into the room carrying two glasses of wine. As he put one down on the table, he held the other to Whoopi's mouth, and she grasped it and took a sip. She put the glass down and they started dancing around the room. At one point, he held her in a tight embrace, and they kissed passionately. I was so paralyzed with excitement that I couldn't breathe. I knew these photos were going to be huge, especially if the other vermin reporters didn't get them as well.

David came back and whispered that the photographer was on the way, and it was okay for us to leave. All during dinner, we were nervous because we didn't know if the paparazzo had gotten the shot or not. It was one thing for us to say we saw Ted and Whoopi kissing, but it was another to have a photo of them doing so. Photos proved to the public what words couldn't.

After dinner, we met with the paparazzo, who told us he had snapped great pictures of Ted and Whoopi kissing, sitting at the dining room table chatting intimately, and dancing wildly in the middle of the living room. Whoopi had put on a big floppy hat and was doing the mambo with Ted. We were thrilled. The paparazzo also told us that he had gotten busted by a security guard. The guard had demanded to know what he was doing at eight o'clock in the evening snapping pictures in the dark. Luckily there was a beautiful rose-covered gazebo nearby and the paparazzo had told the guard that he was taking pictures of it as a possible site for his upcoming wedding. Since the photographer was a registered hotel guest, the guard didn't push the issue.

The paparazzo was ecstatic. Usually, if a photographer is assigned to work on a story for a specific magazine, he is paid a flat rate of $250 a day, whether he gets a photo or not. But if a paparazzo gets a picture on his own time, he can sell the photo to many magazines, thus making himself a tidy bundle. Most paparazzi are able to sell their photos to other magazines without the magazine that hired them knowing about it. It isn't unusual for a photographer to make a cool $25,000 by selling a single photograph to the Australians, Brits, and Italians all in a matter of hours. Even celebrities take advantage of the situation. When Pamela Anderson spontaneously married Tommy Lee, Lee himself sold the wedding photos to the *Enquirer* for a cool $100,000.

We had nailed the photo, but David and I still had to get the full scoop on what was going on between Ted and Whoopi. The next day, we took turns walking past their room, trying to listen in on their conversation. All I could hear was Whoopi's throaty laugh along with classical music in the background. After they left the room late in the day, I peered through the window and saw dozens of roses on the tables, stacks of books on romantic poetry and psychology, and empty bottles of champagne and beer. There was also an open Victoria's Secret box, which led me to believe that Ted had purchased a racy nightgown for Whoopi.

The photographer sat outside Ted's room for nine hours straight, waiting for the couple to come home. A different guard came by and asked him what he was doing. The photographer rubbed his eyes, and said he had gotten into a fight with his girlfriend, and she had kicked him out of their room. He was just sitting on the steps until things blew over. At that moment, I walked by and the paparazzo yelled out my name, told the guard I was his girlfriend, and came running into my arms crying, "I'm so sorry, I'm so sorry."

The next morning, I got up at 7 A.M. As I strolled by Ted's room, I ran smack into Whoopi as she came out of their suite carrying a large overnight bag.

"I'm so sorry," she said. "I wasn't looking where I was going."

"That's all right," I replied. "It's early in the morning, and my eyes aren't even fully open yet. By the way, I'm a big fan of your work. You're an extremely talented lady."

"Thank you. Have a nice day."

She walked away and later returned to the room without the bag. After spotting Whoopi, I immediately reported back to the command post to update David. David and I left our room together and spotted Ted kissing Whoopi good-bye outside their suite. We looked up at the stairs and saw the photographer snapping away. The photos later revealed that Ted wasn't wearing his infamous toupee and the bald spot on his head shined like a newly polished bowling ball. David and I walked by quickly, and Whoopi spotted me and waved. I waved back. The photographer looked at me, puzzled, wondering how Whoopi and I got to be such close buddies.

Later that day, David and I spoke to the room service attendants and found out that Ted and Whoopi had ordered over $1,500 worth of food, champagne, and beer in two days. A local florist revealed that five dozen exotic roses had been sent to their room, along with a card that read,

"To my special rose, I love you." Maids confided to us that Danson was a slob who left his shirt and suits scattered all over the room. They said Whoopi was a funny and charming lady who always gave them big tips when they came to turn down the bed at night. A hotel operator admitted that Danson's wife, Casey, had left many messages for her estranged husband during the course of the week.

The story came together more easily than we had imagined. The next week, the *Star* plastered photos of Ted and Whoopi on the cover, and the story caused a sensation around the country.

9

BITTER FEUDS

**Three Strikes and You're Out
Los Angeles, California
October 1992-January 1993**

I can't pinpoint the exact moment when I went from loving my job at the *Star* to hating it, but I know I began to abhor going into the office toward the end of 1992, and I had been there only a year. I felt stifled and claustrophobic in the tiny quarters that housed the Los Angeles *Star* reporters, so I became creative in my attempts to stay as far away from the office as possible. Sometimes I would say I had to meet a source, other times it was a doctor's appointment, but most often I would say I had gotten a great lead and had to check it out. Then I would usually go home, work on a script or on a book proposal, drug myself with the visual Valium of television, and write a story or two for the *Star.* I actually got more done by being out of the office. As I grew content with my new, self-appointed role as a field reporter, others in the office grew extremely resentful and tried to sabotage my efforts by complaining to the bureau chief. They would say things like, "Why does Lysa get to be out of the office so much? Why is she favored? She's probably at home doing nothing, screwing around, or going shopping. It's not fair!" They were told that as long as I was producing stories, it was none of their business what I was doing.

Their jealousy and cattiness made me sick. They didn't care about each other; they were all out for whatever they could get, even if it meant stepping on a fellow reporter's feet. One reporter named Steve Viens had the nerve to bad-mouth me to David. What did he expect? A nod of agreement about the woman he loved? This sort of thing went on a lot while I was at the magazine.

I stayed on for a few months longer than I planned, then fate stepped in and booted me out the door. It happened during the first week of January, 1993. Bob Smith was away on vacation, and reporter Steve Tinney had assumed the role of office dictator. I was working on a story about Julia Roberts and needed to meet a source of mine for breakfast. I called Steve at home on Monday evening and left word on his answering machine that I would be in the office a bit late on Tuesday because I was meeting my Julia Roberts source. I didn't think it would be a problem, since I met with sources all the time, and this time I wasn't lying.

Steve called me back at 9 P.M. and told me point-blank, "Lysa, you're not to meet your source in the morning, do you hear me? I want you in the office at 9 A.M. sharp."

"What are you talking about? I'm working on a Julia Roberts story and need to meet my source because she can't give me the information over the phone."

"I said, you're not to meet your source in the morning. You're to be in the office by nine, do you hear me?"

"I'm not deaf, Steve. But I don't understand what the problem is."

"You can pull your shit when Bob's in charge, but not when I'm in charge. I won't stand for it. You must, I repeat, must be in the office by nine, or else you'll have to take things up with Steve LeGrice. Do you hear me?"

I ended up saying something to the effect of, "Fuck you, I'm not coming into the office, and I *will* take things up with LeGrice."

Click.

I immediately shot a letter to Steve LeGrice, now the executive editor of the *Star,* voicing my anger over the situation. After LeGrice received the letter, he phoned me and proceeded to shout in my ear, "Why the hell did you fax the letter to the New York office instead of mailing it? Now everyone knows what the fuck is up with you and Tinney. What makes you think you come up with such great stories, anyway?"

My answer was, "If I don't write great stories, then why do you put them on the cover of your magazine?"

He had no answer. He just told me to show up at the office the next morning and pay no attention to Tinney. All I had to do was do my work.

On Tuesday I showed up at 8:50 A.M., spoke briefly with Vicki, the secretary, and started to work on a story. When Steve Tinney walked in, all hell broke loose.

"What are you doing here? Don't you know that you're fired? Go home."

"LeGrice told me to come in today and ignore you, so that's what I'm going to do."

"Get the hell out of here!"

I got on the phone to LeGrice. He asked me to put Tinney on the phone. A minute later, I heard Tinney scream, "She's a liar, and I can't work when she's around. She disrupts the entire office. I will not work with her."

LeGrice told me I wasn't fired, but by that point, I didn't want to work there any longer. After Steve hung up the phone, he started yelling childish remarks at me from his office.

I'd had enough.

I walked up to his door and yelled at the top of my lungs,

"At least I'm not an alcoholic!" I then ran my ass out of the office.

The next morning, I phoned Jim Miteager, the bureau chief at the *Globe,* to inquire about a job. I also called the *Enquirer* and spoke with resident snake Tony Frost. I met with Tony two hours after our phone conversation at Mezzaluna, the trendy Italian restaurant in Brentwood. While I nursed a tropical fruit iced tea, Tony looked through clips of my work and poured on the bull—heavily. He told me he was interested in working with me, but since David worked for the competition and we lived together, it might pose some problems in the area of trust. He said he would think about it and get back to me.

The next day, I met with Jim at the *Globe* and the same problem came up. Because David worked at the competition, I couldn't be offered a staff position; however, Jim was willing to work with me on a freelance basis. I'd heard horror stories about the *Globe* and how they were considered the lowest slimeballs in the tabloid business. *Globe* reporters wanted to be the best and were willing to do anything to get there, including stealing other reporters' stories, phonebooks, sources, notes, and house keys. But I needed work, so I agreed.

During my first week at the *Globe,* I sold four stories at the pretty price of $600 per story plus a $360 lead fee and front-page bonus. The *Globe* printed stories that the *Star* and *Enquirer* were too afraid to touch, ones like, "Soap Star Karen Witter Hooked on Rehab Program" and "Chynna Phillips Anorexia Scare."

Working for the *Globe* felt like working for the CIA. They insisted that I back up all my stories with tape-recorded phone conversations with my sources. I bought a special device that hooked into my phone and used a mini–tape recorder, labeled all my tapes, and sent them to the head office for the lawyers to listen to. Most of my sources agreed to be taped, but the *Globe* encouraged taping without getting prior consent. When I asked Jim about the legality, or rather illegality, of this practice, he assured me that the fine for taping phone calls without the person's prior knowledge was a measly $500.

My stint at the *Globe* didn't last long. The article I wrote about Karen Witter was about to go to print when Jim called me, angry that Karen's publicist had denied everything I wrote in my story. Witter's lawyer even faxed a letter to Jim, stating that if the article about Karen was published, legal action might be taken. This was nothing new. Publicists and lawyers were always threatening to sue the tabloids, but 99 percent of the time they never took action. Since everything I had said in the article was true, I wasn't worried. Jim had a different take on the situation, though. Receiving the letter was a bad sign, he said, and something was definitely wrong. They ran the article anyway, and though Jim never received another threatening letter, that didn't allay his suspicions about me.

The incident blew over, but a week later another one surfaced. I had proposed a story about John Goodman being turned down for life insurance because of his weight. A source had called me a few weeks before I left the *Star* and told me the entire story. He swore it was true and even gave me the name of the insurance company. I had an uneasy feeling about the story but ran with it anyway. Jim did some investigating himself and learned that Goodman was not turned down for insurance in 1993; however, he couldn't prove that Goodman was not turned down for insurance in any other year. But in Jim's mind, I was a liar.

Two strikes. One more and I was out.

A few days later, I was working on a story about Julia Roberts getting her life back together. I had photos of her working out at the Martin Henry Fitness Center, and my angle was that she had hired a nutritionist and was cleaning up her act.

"Untrue," cried Jim.

According to him, Julia was spotted doing cocaine only

a week earlier. I showed him the photos of her at the gym, but he still professed that my story was false.

I challenged him by asking, "How come I never had any problems with my stories at the *Star,* but after only a few weeks at the *Globe,* I run into one problem after another?"

"Maybe I'm an asshole and maybe I'm totally wrong about you," he said.

I silently agreed.

"Nonetheless, I have to fire you," he continued. "Too many things are going wrong, and I can't risk the chance of being sued."

"So that's it?" I asked, incredulous.

"That's it."

"You know, I think you're absolutely right. You are an asshole!"

I went home feeling agitated and angry. I knew my story on Julia wasn't bullshit, and I definitely knew she hadn't been spotted doing coke. I called up Jim and asked him to answer one question: "If you're so convinced that Julia is snorting cocaine instead of cleaning up her life, then why don't you print that?"

No answer from the Peanut Gallery.

I was finally ready to let the issue go.

Enter the *National Enquirer.*

I called Tony Frost and related what had happened and that I was no longer working for the *Globe.* Tony told me about the infamous Tony Castro case a few years back which left the *Globe* wary of potential thieves and liars. Castro, a *Globe* reporter at the time, stole hundreds of thousands of dollars from the publication. His modus operandi was that he would tell the editors he needed cash to pay off a valuable source. He would then fabricate Social Security numbers and names of sources and pocket the cash himself. He would also use his friends' names as sources and rent post office boxes in their names. The money would be sent to these "sources," and Castro would cash the checks and put the money into secret bank accounts. His wife was also believed to be involved in the scam. Castro was eventually arrested and served time in prison.

The *Enquirer* took me on as a freelance reporter and from day one, I worked like a dog. Tony Frost called me almost daily to go on stakeouts, check out leads, and work on stories. From the very beginning, he treated me like a lady. He asked a lot of personal questions about David and me, but I assured him I never gave my information to the competition. The money was great—$150 a day plus a story and lead fee if I came up with the idea. I didn't have the hassle of being tied down to an office and didn't have to report my whereabouts every minute of the day. The only scary part was living paycheck to paycheck, but I was willing to risk that in exchange for my freedom. It was a well-known fact that *Enquirer* reporters were paid more and treated better than *Star* reporters. I knew it the minute I stepped into the *Enquirer*'s plush Sunset Boulevard office. The reporters' desks were gigantic and each had its own computer. *Star* reporters had to share computers in the back of the tiny office, and we often had to wait hours until a computer was free.

As I became more successful working with the *Enquirer,* Bob Smith from the *Star* called me and asked if I had any information about Justine Bateman. He assured me he would pay top dollar if I could gather details about her romantic life and her battle with her weight. I asked if I could work for both the *Star* and the *Enquirer,* and he told me I could do whatever I wanted since I was freelance, but I couldn't sell the same story to both magazines. When I asked him why he suddenly decided he wanted to work with me again, he replied, "After you left the *Star,* you swore to me you wouldn't reveal our secrets and sources to the competition, and as far as I know, you've kept your word. I don't care what happened between you and Steve Tinney, you're a good reporter, and I want to work with you again. Just lay low for a while and talk only to me about stories. If Steve is in charge when I'm away, refer your stories to Dick in New York."

I agreed to work freelance for the *Star* again, and within three weeks I was making double what I made when I worked for them full-time. It was strange working for both the *Enquirer* and the *Star* since they were now owned by the same company. The competition for stories between the two rags was great, and I was constantly offered bribes to spill the beans on what the other magazine was working. Because David was still on staff at the *Star,* I didn't want to jeopardize his position by double-dealing, so I decided to play it straight and not leak any information.

Tony Frost would often page me when I was out of town and try to squeeze out information on whatever story I was working for the *Star.* He was a competitive fellow who couldn't stand having the other rags beat him to the punch. He offered me money, a full-time on-staff position at the *Enquirer,* and lots of prestige, but I knew he was full of shit. I told him, "Tony, if I rat on the *Star* for you, what makes you think I won't rat on the *Enquirer* for the *Star* at some point? A liar is a liar is a liar."

He finally backed off and found another reporter at the *Star* to bribe. In this business, reporters are loyal to whomever has the biggest checkbook.

Until the spring of 1990, both the Enquirer *and the* Star *were separate entities, run by quixotic press barons, throwbacks to jazz-age journalism. The* Enquirer *was originally owned by Generoso Pope, who, when Princess Grace died in a car accident in 1982, dispatched a chartered Learjet full of teams of crack reporters and $500,000 per team with orders to cover every aspect of the story. One team spent over $100,000 on reenacting the accident, buying a brand-new Rolls-Royce identical to Grace's for the sole purpose of chucking it off the same cliff and taking pictures of it as it crashed end over end.*

The Star *was Rupert Murdoch's cash cow, having one*

quarter the staff of the Enquirer *but rivaling it in circula-*
tion. One summer, the Star *had made a deal with a young*
boytoy (Blaise Tostie) of a prominent country-and-western
singer (Dolly Parton) to tell all for $200,000, only to bury
the story so as not to disturb negotiations between Parton
and Murdoch's Fox TV for Dolly's new variety show. Barry
Levine, Star*'s then bureau chief, and "Big" Bill Dick,*
Star*'s crazed news editor, had gone hog-wild on the story,*
treating Blaise like a Mob witness being hunted by invisible
legions of Gambino family gunmen. They hid him in a suite
at the Four Seasons Hotel under a fake name. They hired a
limo with blacked-out windows to ferry him from the hotel
to the office. One time, convinced they were being stalked
by the competition's paparazzi, they hustled Blaise into the
backseat with a blanket over his head. The limo laid a patch
of smoking rubber and fishtailed out of the hotel parking
lot, its door swinging wildly until a hard right turn closed
it. These ridiculous efforts were enacted so the competition
wouldn't have a picture of the kid to run alongside the most
dreaded journalistic parry between the deadly tabloid ri-
vals: the same-week "spoiler story" that pokes holes in all
your overblown prose.

Barry was morose for weeks after Murdoch ordered the
story killed, and ascribed Dick's death weeks later to "a
broken heart."

We were the Visigoths of Murdoch's burgeoning multi-
media empire, a fact driven home at an informal cocktail
gathering of us and his other magazines. The well-bred,
well-dressed, soft-spoken staffers of Premiere, TV Guide,
and Auto *magazine recoiled as we entered in a pack. We*
were loud, obnoxious, drunken, vicious, uncontrollable
brutes. I felt like putting on a spiked helmet, smashing
crockery, swilling wine, and making crude passes at the
waitresses.

We were extreme because we had to be. We had to beat
the Enquirer *with bigger, better, and meaner stories, sto-*
ries that would make the homemakers of America soil their

pantyhose in the checkout aisles, make their pudgy fingers tremble as they snatched the Star *out of the wire basket and stuffed it between the turkey pot pies and the Ho-Ho's.*

Every Monday, both issues hit the stands. Every Monday, the unseen editors in New York went over the magazines with a fine-tooth comb, comparing our dirt with theirs for flavor, consistency, and venom.

The editors of both papers were Brits who had cut their teeth on the ferociously competitive Fleet Street tabs, then come to America to take advantage of the wide-open field and easy money. They all knew one another from "back when" and needled one another over their successes and failures. A bad showing on a major story meant they would have to face the prospect of eating crow the next time they all gathered at the pub to lie and brag and fondle one another's bum.

Consequently, a reporter who missed out on seemingly trivial details ("Why didn't you get the color of Roseanne's wedding bouquet? Why didn't you know Lisa Marie ate a quart of fudge ripple ice cream a night while she was pregnant?") often sat under a dark, gloomy cloud all Monday afternoon, afraid to pick up the phone to hear about yet another failure. Too many failures, and one day you arrive at work to find your desk cleaned out and your possessions waiting by the receptionist in a cheap cardboard box.

But a reporter whose story contained more bizarre, kooky, wacky, adjective-laden descriptions of celebrity excess and melodramatic emotions sat confidently, head held high. And far above him or her, wreathed in a golden nimbus of glory, was the reporter who brought in a scoop, a revelation of celeb misconduct and woe that the competition totally missed. Such a feat made the reporter bulletproof for the next three or four months. He or she could loaf and rest on his or her laurels while the other reporters scurried doing follow-ups and sidebars to the big opus. This reporter might also be awarded with the next all-expenses paid trip to a sun-drenched tropical isle, and if the reporter played his or her cards right and threatened to go to the competition, he or she might even receive a promotion.

On a day-to-day level, this atmosphere fostered a sense of intrigue, treachery, and backbiting reminiscent of the Borgias. We didn't cover stories. We went to war.

If we spotted the competition sitting in a car at the same stakeout, we would distract them while a confederate let the air out of their tires or shoved a potato in their tailpipe. Or we might phone the DMV and report their car as stolen. Car chases were Mad Max free-for-alls, as rental cars full of paparazzi and reporters ran each other off the road, took shortcuts across lawns and backyards, and violated every traffic ordinance on the books. One senior reporter supposedly loved getting blowjobs from his comely co-worker while screeching around corners and running red lights in pursuit of Sean Penn and Madonna, until he was paparazzi'd by a competitor, and the photos were sent to his superiors.

If we knew other reporters were in the same hotel, we'd call the manager, pretending to be them, and act drunk and curse him out, hoping to get the competition tossed out. The best trick of all was to intercept their phone messages and call their sources, convincing them to switch sides, or pretend to be a private eye investigating them and warning them not to sell their stories.

Many scurvy reporters supplemented their income as moles for the competition, calling former colleagues on other magazines and tipping them off to hot stories. They were the most hated creatures in the business, traitorous rodents who sold out their colleagues' stories and sources, and their unseen, but always felt, presence contributed to the paranoid atmosphere. You could always tell if a reporter had a hot story on the phone because his end of the conversation got very vague. Or maybe everyone in the office was just closing drug deals.

In our spare hours, we would disguise our voices and call the competition's office, pretending to be a tipster with *a hot story, hoping to lure them into committing a team of reporters on a bogus story while we went after the real deal.*

My first out-of-town assignment was just such a story: I was sent to Twentynine Palms, a fly speck in the Mojave Desert, on a tip that Liz Taylor was drying out in a private spa. Thrilled, I rented a convertible, met up with paparazzo Peter Brandt, and headed out at ninety-five miles an hour, convinced I was onto something big. Somewhere along the way, the road became gravel. Then dirt. Then ruts. Finally, we were inching along a dusty trail forty miles deep in the desert. At last we reached the address where Liz was supposed to be.

A sun-bleached shack leaned to one side against a giant saguaro. One wall had been ripped ragged by a shotgun blast. The roof sagged in the middle like a swaybacked horse. A broken clothesline dangled dirty shirts in the dust.

"If Liz is here, it's the biggest tabloid story of the last fifty years. Hell, it's the biggest story, period," I commented, surveying the scene. A four-foot-tall, 200-pound woman and three wide-eyed children ambled out from behind the tumbleweeds. "Hi," I said. "Bet you don't get too many visitors this far out."

"Nah," she spat. "You're the second bunch out here in the last two weeks. Before that, we hadn't seen no strangers for nearly two years."

I had a sinking feeling. "What were the other guys doing out here?" I asked as visions of a desert Deliverance *danced in my head.*

"They was from some magazine and they said they was looking for Liz Taylor. I figured they was DEA till they gave me their card."

She handed me the card. I looked at the sweat-darkened rectangle of paper. It was from a reporter for the Globe. *Some smart-ass* Enquirer *reporter had tricked both magazines. I looked at Brandt, who had his head bowed and was*

*rubbing his aching kidneys. "Let's get the hell out of here,"
he muttered.*

*A total waste of time, effort and money? Not really. The
Star was selling 3.8 million copies a week, with one million
copies as the break-even point. That meant Murdoch took
home $2.2 million a week in pure profit. But sometimes
$2.2 million just isn't enough.*

*Profits from the Star allowed Murdoch to buy 20th Cen-
tury-Fox, start Fox TV and British Sky Broadcasting, pay
$3 billion for TV Guide, and acquire book publishing giant
HarperCollins. The debt load was crushing, however.
Small things started to crop up. Some Fridays there were
no paychecks. Payments to snitches were late, lost, or ignored. Expenses took months and months to recover. It
was the rattle of small stones dislodging before the ava-
lanche.*

*One spring morning we came into the office to a strange
quietness. The bureau chief's office door was closed. We sat
down and began combing the morning gossip columns for
tidbits we could try to work into larger stories. All at once,
Barry's door flew open, and he rushed out and pinned a
typewritten piece of paper to the bulletin board, then
rushed back into his office and slammed the door. We
looked at one another in trepidation. This kind of behavior
was usually reserved only for notices of extreme dread, like
major lawsuits or mass firings.*

*The notice said: "A decision regarding the future of Star
magazine will be announced in an hour. Upper manage-
ment has been involved in negotiations with an unnamed
party."*

*Barry had given his heart and soul to the Star, coming
in at 7 A.M. and not leaving until midnight, if indeed he left
at all. He worked every weekend, no matter what. He was
involved in every story from start to finish and read every
word before it was sent to the editors. The prospect of the
company going under terrified him.*

We knocked softly on Barry's door and entered to find

him on the verge of tears, hands shaking as he poured whis-
key from a little airline bottle into his coffee mug. Six or
seven little plastic bottles lay tipped over, staining his blot-
ter. "What's happening?" we asked. Barry just shook his
head, unable to speak.

Barry loved chaos, loved shouting, disorder, anger, fear,
insults, stress, deadlines, snap decisions, all the classic in-
gredients of a newsroom. If things were too sedate, he
would stir them up. He explored people's personalities
until he found the buttons that would set them off, then he
would smash the buttons with a sledgehammer, stand
back, and watch the fireworks. It not only was entertaining
but kept the reporters on their toes. For Barry to be intimi-
dated by chaos and uncertainty was a bad sign.

A call from New York came in. He ordered us out. Ten
minutes later he emerged and posted another bombshell on
the board. "The Star *has been sold to the* Enquirer *group."*
We were stunned. The Hatfields had bought out the Mc-
Coys. The Palestine Liberation Organization had taken
over Israel.

It was all because of some satellite dishes rotting in
warehouses. In England, most people had access to only
four channels on their TVs: BBC 1, 2, 3, and 4. Murdoch
figured there was a huge untapped market for the hundreds
of channels Americans routinely cruise through on cable
every night. But rather than installing miles and miles of
cable, he wanted to avoid dealing with sticky town councils
and installers' unions by selling satellite dishes on a grand
scale and beaming down Fox programs and movies to a
starved mass audience.

Murdoch invested hundreds of millions in the dishes and
technical facilities. It was about as popular as a naked
ninety-eight-year-old poolside at the Playboy mansion.

It was also at this time that the world economy went
into the toilet, advertising spending plummeted about 30
percent, and the balloon payments on Murdoch's $3 billion
TV Guide *buyout started coming due.*

Murdoch needed cash, and he needed it fast. The Star *was steady. Profitable. Required little attention.*

The rumored price for the Star *was $400 million and an additional $400 million in stock.*

In the newsroom, we were crushed. The rug had been pulled out from under us. We were now the playthings of our most hated enemies, delivered by the hands of our superiors. We could hear their laughter ringing in our ears as we got reports that at Enquirer *headquarters in Lantana, Florida, they were ordering cases of Dom Perignon to celebrate their stunning final victory over the* Star.

One last act of defiance was left. Volatile reporter Alvin Grimes was fuming. "I'm calling the Ice Pick," he declared, referring to the Enquirer *editor nicknamed after the weapon employed on the unprotected backs of unsuspecting victims.*

"Do it," we all said.

He dialed. "Can I speak to Iain Calder, please? Tell him it's Bill calling."

He waited. We wondered what he was going to say. I figured he would chicken out and hang up. "Iain? Iain Calder?" he asked. "FUUUUUCK YOUUUUU!" He slammed the phone down.

We erupted in cheers and laughter.

It's been downhill ever since.

10

UNNATURAL DISASTERS

Shake, Rattle, and Roll
San Francisco, California
October 1989

I had been infiltrating the set of Back to the Future
III *in Sonora, where an elaborate Western town
had been built in the middle of nowhere, hundreds
of miles from the traditional studio lots in Los Angeles. The
thinking was that once the movie was wrapped, they could
more than recoup their $1 million investment in the set by
renting it out to other shoots. A good idea, as it turned out,
as it has since been used for the 1992–1993 wave of west-
erns, including* Unforgiven *and* Tombstone.

Unfortunately, in the first week of the Back to the Future
III *shoot, some oxen broke loose and wrecked a good deal
of the flimsy storefronts. Filming was delayed at least two
weeks. Japanese investors had pumped more than $100
million into shooting the two sequels back to back, and because* Back to the Future II *hadn't yet been released, they*

hadn't seen a dollar of their investment returned. They were swarming on the set, worried and tense, keeping tabs on how all their money was being spent.

The story we were trying to verify came from a sleazy local private investigator and a wacked-out casting assistant who tried to sell me a script about how she was kidnapped by aliens out of the trunk of her car. She kept carrying on about how Close Encounters of the Third Kind *was ripped off from her idea, and she wanted revenge on Spielberg. One of the problems about sources is that sometimes they turn sour and start giving you information just because they want someone to listen to their shit.*

Anyway, I had driven up to Sonora in a rented hot-rod Cadillac. I was feeling frisky for the open road and wanted to see the scenery around Big Sur, so on October 17 I told the bureau chief I was going to take the day off and drive back to Los Angeles.

I drove up the east side of the San Francisco Bay on the I-880 near Oakland. Then I crossed the Bay Bridge, took the 101 to Watsonville, hit the Pacific Coast Highway, and continued south. At dusk somewhere south of Santa Cruz, the car began hopping up and down on the road like a pogo stick. Since it was a rental, I didn't think too much of it, other than say to myself, "Damn, these Caddies' suspensions are for shit. The front end is catching air as if it were some cholo's hydraulic-jacked lowrider." When I tried to tune in to some San Fran radio stations, all I got was static. I figured the mountains were blocking out the signal.

It wasn't until I got to San Luis Obispo, where the streets were full of emergency vehicles and panicked people, that I began to sense something was amiss. I pulled over to ask what the commotion was. I was told there had been a 6.9 earthquake, and it was feared that the nuclear reactor dome at Diablo Canyon, which was built right on a major fault, might have cracked. I smelled a story.

I called the office and was told, "You moron. San Francisco has been devastated. The bureau chief, Donna, Julian, and Alvin chartered the last jet out of Santa Monica, beating out CBS, to fly in. Get your ass back up there."

I was expected to go into an area of flattened, smoking rubble, where dazed, bloody, dirty survivors who had clawed their way out from under tons of rubble wandered through unsanitary water. It sounded heavenly, full of the pain and pathos that make a great news story. I bought gallons of Evian, remembering my grand-uncle's stories of typhus from polluted water when he was in the big San Francisco quake of 1906. I also bought beef jerky, cigarettes, and alcohol. I figured with that great a societal dislocation, the locals might be on a barter economy for a while. Then I strapped myself in and opened up the V-8 on the freeway heading north.

It was eerie. The quake had knocked out all the lights, and it looked like I was heading into a big black hole. I could see by the moonlight that there were towns on each side of the road, but they were all dark. No one else was on the road. I felt like the Omega Man, that bad Charlton Heston movie in which he plays the last man alive on earth.

I got to Watsonville. Only four hours earlier it had been a little artichoke-farming town. Now it looked like a Bosch painting of hell. The quake and the hundred or so aftershocks that hit that night had wrenched open gas mains, and the flaming houses lit the otherwise pitch-black streets. People streamed out carrying valuables. I saw a woman stagger past with a VCR and a teddy bear under her arm. Strange, the things people grab when they have to flee. I tried to get out to take a picture, but National Guardsmen, unnerved by the panic, starting waving their arms and guns in my direction. I guess they were afraid of looters. I asked a cop about the roads to San Francisco and was told that some overpasses had collapsed and I could make it only if I had a four-wheel drive. I tried going up the twisting mountain roads, but on one particularly violent aftershock, the pavement cracked open ahead of me. I decided to go back into town and wait till morning.

The next day I called my office and found that the Star *crew had checked into the Oakland Hyatt, right next to where the double-decker freeway had pancaked, flattening rush-hour commuters in their cars. I got to the hotel, got a room, and was immediately teamed up with Bob Smith, the legendary brawling, hard-drinking Scotsman who worked out of New York at the time. Reporters Donna Balancia and Alvin Grimes were to go to the Fisherman's Wharf area, where many of the houses of the rich and famous had been destroyed. Alvin claimed he had had a relapse of malaria, and in truth he was pale, clammy, and running a fever.*

Bob and I walked out to the collapsed freeway. I could tell we were heading for the real shit, because TV satellite trucks were lined up for blocks and the streets around the giant concrete ramps were blocked off with that yellow POLICE LINE DO NOT CROSS *tape. Evidently, some of the neighborhood sweethearts had been out between the two levels, robbing the dead and not-so-dead, looting watches from severed wrists, and so forth. At least that's what the cops said. Bob was like a force of nature, determined to get right into the thick of things. I knew we were headed for trouble because the cops were having to deal with a lot of disaster tourists and were trying to keep them from getting too close to the scene. They were letting only reporters with official credentials pass. This was a problem, because the* Star *is not thought of too highly in law enforcement circles, and we had been refused press passes.*

We worked out a strategy: I would run up to the cops with my obvious reporter's notebook in hand and ask some dumb question while Bob trundled past. Then I would hurry after him, not waiting for the reply. Don't even give the cops time to think or question, just act like, "Of course we belong here." You'd be surprised how far the right attitude will carry you. If you act like you know what you're doing, people very rarely will bother you.

Anyway, we wanted to get up close to the action, so we kept heading north, parallel to the freeway, past checkpoint *after checkpoint. We found a warehouse owner who would allow us on the roof to shoot pictures for $100, right after NBC got done.*

Not good enough.

We kept going into the night, into neighborhoods best described as scary. Locals were screaming at us, "Get out of here, you dipshit! They're going to kill your ass, white boy!" Eventually we found a dead-end street with no cops that ended right next to the overpass. A staggering, weaving junkie was charging the locals twenty-five cents for access to his backyard full of rusty bedsprings, tin cans, and offal so that they could see over his fence. Bob slipped the guy five dollars and his eyes bugged out of his head. He sprang to his feet and ran off. We saw giant jackhammers breaking up the pavement so rescue workers could crawl in and get people out of cars in which they had been trapped for more than twenty-four hours. We stood on top of an old radiator and strained for a closer look. The stench of dead meat hit our nostrils, and I saw torn-off human limbs being pulled out of the rubble and twisted steel. I looked at Bob. "This is gruesome. We gotta get shots of this."

We headed back to find a shooter. On the front stoop, the owner sat, totally fried. He had already traded the five dollars for a fix and was ebullient. "Ya come back here anytime. Anytime at all. Look all you want." I felt eyes on us the whole way out.

The pictures we eventually got from the backyard were sent to New York and rejected for being too graphic for our readers.

The first week's coverage—that there had been a terrible earthquake and accounts of the devastation—was already on the presses. We now had to cull the best stories of the survivors: the worst damage, the luckiest escape, the most heart-wrenching tragedy, the unlucky victim who ignored advice and paid the price, the hero who sacrificed so others would live, and so on.

The only problem was that every other media outlet in

North America was there, too, trying to come up with the
exact same things. Classic pack journalism mentality. And
when it takes a week for our stories to hit the newsstands
and only an hour for TV to go coast to coast, our disadvan-
tage couldn't be more obvious. The only way we could compete was by throwing around larger sums of money. The
Los Angeles Times *had over seventy-five reporters there,
more than the entire staffs of large dailies, with two assistants whose only job was to supply them with live batteries
for their cell phones. It was guerrilla warfare. Fifty or so
reporters would push and jostle in a holding pen near the
freeway, constantly trying to get cops aside for exclusive
interviews and story leads. The press quickly focused on
the story of Julio Berumen, a young boy who survived the
freeway collapse. They had to cut his aunt in half with a
chainsaw to get to him, then amputated his leg to free him.
A "miracle baby" story.*

*Donna Balancia and Barry Levine went to the hospital
where Julio was being kept and found forty reporters already kicked out of the area. Donna bribed two orderlies
$100 apiece to cover her with a sheet and sneak her in on
a gurney. Soon she was sitting alongside Julio's uncle, trying to set up an interview, when Barry arrived. He had
sneaked in through a fire entrance and was screaming on a
cell phone. His hair was standing on end, and he stuck out
like a sore thumb. The cops arrived to give them both the
bum's rush.*

*I was sent with paparazzo Jim Knowles to Julio's ele-
mentary school, where I lied to a nun, telling her I was
from CBS so she would give me the last photo of Julio. The
photo desk in New York told Knowles they wanted him to
blow it up to life size and shoot the neighbors holding the
picture and crying. He hung up the cell phone and shook
his head. "That has got to be the stupidest idea I've ever
heard. They're not going to cooperate. A photo of a photo
of a photo. How bogus can you get?"*

Meanwhile, Julian was harassing Tom Brokaw as he was

preparing to go live nationwide. "Tom! Don't you remember me? Julian? The '72 Republican Convention in Miami?" Brokaw snubbed him, so Julian vowed revenge and shot photos of Brokaw blow-drying and styling his hair on the trunk of his limo in front of a group of newly homeless waiting in a breadline.

Knowles was also sent south to the Santa Cruz epicenter to shoot a hole in the ground. That's right, shoot a picture of a dirt pit and make it exciting. It was a crevasse that had opened up during the quake, and it was the deepest in the area. Somehow Knowles convinced neighbors to stand at the bottom of the pit and point up at their house. The entire time they were down there, the woman was crying because she was convinced the crack was going to close back up and bury her alive.

I was assigned to go to Haight-Ashbury to try to find old hippies who had slept through the quake or who thought it was some kind of bad acid trip. Expecting love beads and flowers, instead I found a Gap store and BMW-driving yuppies.

Barry decided to pull out all the stops and get an exclusive with Julio. He and Donna went to the family's house and began ringing the bell maniacally. No one answered. He went to a window, where he could see the father and his brother sitting inside. Barry began shouting and waving money.

"I've got $5,000 here. Sell me your son's story. I've got $5,000. You can make a profit off all this."

A voice came out, "Get that shit out of here."

Barry turned to Donna and said, "That's not the best way to open negotiations."

Alvin and I were in Barry's nineteenth-floor hotel room watching college football. We had been working from dawn to dusk and were taking a break. We had ordered huge breakfasts and rounds of cocktails and charged them to Barry's room. The game was interrupted by the announcement that a survivor had been pulled from the I-880 after six days. Just as our food arrived, Barry charged in, worked up from the Berumen fiasco. "Uh, Barry," I said. "We just heard they found another survivor."

That was all he needed to go off. "You guys are loafing here while the biggest story of the whole quake goes on only a block away? What the hell are you doing here?"

"We're hungry. We haven't eaten yet." I was shoveling down huevos rancheros and guzzling a screwdriver. Barry had been saving all the earthquake clips from local papers, and I was using them as a placemat.

"Take your Spanish omelet and get the hell down there!" Barry raged.

I threw on a coat and went out to stand with the rest of the pack in a pouring rainstorm for hours while police and rescuers gave us dribs and drabs of information. That was when I first began to hate TV reporters contemptuously. We were interviewing the muscular blond paramedic who had found "Lucky" Buck Helm, asking how he was rescued, what shape he was in, if he said anything, and other details. We were shouted down by brain-damaged TV weasels who asked her four times to spell her name. Finally she just walked off in disgust.

I was soaked to the bone. The ink on my notepad had run into a soggy, unreadable mass. It was a real zoo.

At the same time, Bob Smith was heading north to Buck's hometown to talk to his relatives. With true Star luck, he stumbled on the craziest one of all, Buck's drunken, crippled, ne'er-do-well biker son and his horrific girlfriend, whom we dubbed Mountain Girl. Bob handed them a wad of cash, got them drunk, drove them to Oakland, and put them up in the suite next to Barry's.

The next morning, I received a curt phone call from Barry ordering me to come up to his room. I got off the elevator and saw the hallway was full of broken glass. I knocked on Barry's door and saw it snap open and catch on the chain. A reddened, fearful eyeball looked me over.

"Shh," Barry hushed, ushering me into the disheveled room.

"What the hell happened here?" I asked.

Buck's barbarian relatives decided to do it up on the Star, ordered hundred-dollar bottles of rare whiskey, and got drunk and unruly. About midnight, Mountain Girl came to Barry's room with her clothes half torn off and her face red and blotchy. She said Buck's son was drunk and had beaten her with his cane, which he had used ever since he crashed his Harley. Barry went over to try to keep the peace. "Why were you hitting her?"

"I was watching a porn movie on the TV, and it made me feel like beating her," Biker Boy said thickly.

That morning I received a call requesting that I drive Buck's son and Mountain Girl to the hospital where Buck was recovering and get a picture. I was to restrain them if another brawl developed, but not to rough them up so much that they got mad and refused to cooperate. The first thing they did when they got in the car was to demand we drive around Oakland looking for drug dealers so they could score some coke. "I can't face all this unless I got a head fulla' blow," Biker Boy mumbled.

Alvin and I exchanged rueful looks. Here we go again. We were becoming the Dirty Harrys of the Star. Every dirty job, we got it.

I improvised. "I'm sorry, I don't know where to go to score, man. We're kind of on a strict schedule, so I think we better go to the hospital first and get the story and photo and then Barry will give you thousands of dollars and you can get a lot more blow with that than we ever could."

I just wanted to get the story out of them, then dump them with the money and not have to deal with Ozzie and Harriet meet the Mansons. At the hospital, Alvin and I sat on the sidewalk with Mountain Girl and tried to keep her from getting hysterical. Biker Boy eventually chickened out of shooting a picture of his old man as he lay in his hospital bed. (Buck died two months later from the damage done to *his renal system from six days without water.) So we had to make do with yellowed photos of Buck and his pet goat.*

On our last night in town, Barry got clearance from New York to take us all out to a fancy dinner as a reward. We had been in the area for about two weeks, and we all looked pretty scruffy. We got turned away from two restaurants and wound up at a fancy seafood place near the wharf. Alvin ordered two lobsters and I had a $50 appetizer. I remember having my own $400 bottle of Cristal champagne, and Bob handing me $75 shots of port at the end of the meal.

The whole operation had been a Roman Empire of excess. We had had nine reporters and four photographers working on the story for two weeks, all of us ordered to get an exclusive deal no matter what the cost. It was a heady feeling, a sense of having total free rein, able to go off on gonzo kamikaze quests and get into trouble all in the name of getting the story. New York was pulling out all the stops. If we had wanted to charter a guided missile frigate to take pictures of the cracks in the underside of the Bay Bridge, we would have been indulged.

After our feast, in true Fear and Loathing fashion, Alvin and I decided to see some decadent San Francisco nightlife. Unfortunately, we asked a gay cabbie where to find lots of women and wound up at a lesbian disco. Hours later, in some North Beach hellhole, we made the mistake of asking for the strongest shot they had. They gave us an Atomic Bomb, straight 151 rum and Tabasco sauce. Alvin downed the shot, immediately turned white as a sheet, and headed straight for the bathroom to do the heave-ho.

On the ride back to the hotel, Alvin was hanging out the window of the cab, puking over the side of the fog-bound Golden Gate bridge while the militant driver tried to convince us that the earthquake was just another instrument of the ruling classes to exterminate the ghettos. Like AIDS. And crack. And high-cholesterol fast-food restaurants that serve animal flesh cultivated at the expense of the beautiful rain forests. I argued for a time until I began to fear the cabbie would drive us into a politically correct ambush where Greenpeace fanatics would club us fascist sympathizers to death like baby harp seals. A ridiculous, paranoid notion, but that's what San Francisco does to you. It's so fringe that anything seems possible.

"This town deserves what it got," I muttered as Alvin puked lobster onto the passing heaps of broken bricks and twisted steel reinforcing rods.

Travels With Skinhead
Kingman, Arizona
April 1995

It has always been a hard and fast rule of mine to avoid tangling with law enforcement whenever possible, a lesson I learned when a jacked-up Beverly Hills cop almost shot me in the head for reaching for a paperback book.

But when I was assigned to investigate the background of Timothy McVeigh immediately after the Oklahoma City bombing, I found once again that covering breaking news stories is as dangerous and Machiavellian as anything Hollywood can offer. At the end of a week in McVeigh's hometown of Kingman, Arizona—home of militias, neo-Nazis, survivalists, revolutionaries, paranoiacs, and flat-out, bat-crazy lunatics—I had been stranded in the desert with a skinhead punk, threatened by bull-necked wanna-be GI Joes, and spied on by the FBI.

I had a pretty good idea what I was heading into as I wheeled the rental car down the barren highway from Las Vegas to Kingman, a tiny, sun-scorched desert city set amid rugged mountain terrain that looked like it was blasted out of the rock with a blowtorch. I knew that cops, federal investigators, and other reporters would be crawling all over the place and that I would have to do something very *extreme to come up with a nugget of information that hadn't already been reported live coast to coast on CNN.*

And from my days working at the Arizona Republic, *I knew Kingman had always been a center for disgruntled, even radical individualists, the kind of people who just can't stand other people. In short, people who would react to an interview request from a funny-looking out-of-town reporter in much the same way a pit bull reacts to an attempt to grab away its favorite soup bone.*

McVeigh had found a home here.

Star *wanted me to come up with an ex-girlfriend or best buddy to talk about McVeigh's personal life, to tell how and why he allegedly got to the point where blowing up buildings with homemade bombs and killing hundreds of innocent people seemed like a good idea. I figured anyone who knew anything about McVeigh was either in custody already or was shit-scared and holed up in the hills. I decided the best thing to do would be to get what we call the local color, a description of anything or anyone noteworthy or unusual in the area, to use as background, as a way of understanding and providing insight into the life McVeigh led. I hoped I would be able to find something in this glorified truck stop.*

As it turned out, it was harder to find someone or something that didn't relate to the bombing. The first thing I saw driving into town (after getting nailed in a speedtrap— "Fourth reporter we got today," chortled the deputy) was a military surplus store called Archie's Bunker. The next thing I saw was a couple of twitchy bearded guys wearing battle fatigues and driving a pickup truck with a large rifle rack in the rear window.

"Looks like we got some live ones here," I said to myself as I pulled up to a media swarm of a dozen TV trucks parked in front of the local courthouse. Most often, a reporter's best source is other reporters, because they have a different viewpoint on the story, and in quid pro quo fashion, you can trade them what you have for information they

have that will fill in holes in your story. Such was not the case this time, however. The TV crews were there, badgering the curious but puzzled locals, asking about rumors that someone was going to blow up the courthouse in Kingman.

I bailed out on the sidewalk weenie roast and victim-hunt and went in search of a decent hotel to get out of the relentless sun and quaff a beer. I found that Kingman is full of nothing but cheap motels for truckers caught between L.A. and Phoenix who don't have enough crank to make it another six hours. As I was checking in, the desk clerk eyed me up and down through her unfiltered Lucky Strike haze and snorted, " 'nuther city-boy writer here to get a piece of the big story, huh? Sure. I got just the room fer you."

I drove past the algae-scummed pool and rows of Winnebagos and suddenly began to appreciate her cruel joke. Lined up side by side were five nondescript four-door sedans with tiny hubcaps, big antennas, and roll-bar suspensions. Like a Mexican bandito in a Humphrey Bogart film, the cars scream "Los Federales" at the tops of their lungs.

My only previous experience dealing with the FBI in the field was when Washington, D.C., mayor Marion Barry had been busted for smoking crack, entrapped (he claimed) by an L.A.-based model. I had been staking out her apartment along with a TV crew when cars just like the ones here in Kingman started sneaking around the block. I immediately fired up my car and drove off to the hoots and derision of the TV crew. Fifteen minutes later, I cruised by and saw the crew handcuffed, lying on their bellies on the burning asphalt, screaming impotently as stone-faced FBI agents yanked the tape out of their cameras and threw all their gear out of their trucks.

The next morning I got up early and tried to talk to the agents as they were getting into their cars. I was greeted with unbridled comtempt and hostility.

"Can you tell me how the investigation is going? Are you

making progress? Have you identified any accomplices?" I asked.

"Investigation? What investigation? There is no investigation going on here," a buzz-cut, flinty-eyed pit-bull-in-a-suit spat. "Who are you? Where are you from? What are you doing here?"

Heads were swiveling. Other agents were gliding in to surround me and flexing their knees into the "deadly pounce" position. In a second, I was going to be at the bottom of a mass of meat and gristle, with forearms locked around my windpipe, knees crushing my groin, and fists wrenching my arms out of their sockets.

I raised my hands and backed away, making sure my pen and notebook were in plain sight. "Hey, ease up, guys, I'm a reporter. Press. I was just wondering if you guys could give me a couple of quotes, maybe let me tag along if you're going to be making any arrests."

I handed the agent my business card. He relaxed fractionally but shook his head in disgust and exasperation. "First of all, no quotes. Call the Phoenix office and ask for the Special Agent in Charge for that. And second, if I or my men see you trying to follow us around, your ass is grass. Now get the hell out of here."

Friendly guys.

They watched me walk back to my room, eyes swiveling like the gyro-stabilized turrets on an M-1 tank. My next step was to get the local newspaper and try to figure out the lay of the local sociological land.

It made for interesting reading. In 1987, members of the Arizona Patriots, a heavily armed white supremacist group, were arrested in Kingman while plotting to blow up a bank and steal the money to finance their movement. Right-wing groups, attracted to the solitude and space, find the desert an ideal, convenient place to conduct paramilitary training and live without interference. Driving around and conducting man-in-the-street interviews, I quickly learned that *there was a wide spectrum of bad-asses roaming the bad-lands, including:*

- *survivalists, who believe society is going to collapse in a great disaster and who just want to be left alone on their isolated ranches, eating canned food and only shooting people who trespass on their territory.*
- *the Arizona Patriots, who believe the country has been taken over by weak communists who want to take away their guns and give their money to welfare.*
- *white supremacists, who arm themselves for a race war they feel is inevitable and who ride around in pickup trucks looking for minorities to insult and beat up.*
- *neo-Nazis, or Fourth Reich skinheads, who plan to establish the Nazi form of government in the United States by destabilizing the current government through acts of terror. They are the most prone to violence, since they believe that every such act brings them closer to their goal. They target anyone not meeting their ideal of racial purity, especially Jews, blacks, homosexuals, and intellectuals.*

The radical groups have their own newspaper, the Mohave Report, which contains columns that call for the deaths of inferior peoples. One column said, "Danger is nature's way of eliminating the stupid. Without safety, stupid people die in accidents. With safety, we are devolving into half-witted mutants, because idiots who by all rights should be dead are spared from their rightful early graves and are free to breed even more imbeciles."

Looking at the depth and breadth of the intellectual discourse displayed in the paper, I broke into hysterical laughter because the drooling pinhead writers and readers would be the first on the execution list, were their own policies followed. Talk about a blind spot. The Report also blathered on about the Iron Heel of Government and the New World Order, and complained about how they should be free to live without taxes and the evils of government interference.

Armed with a growing sense of paranoia, I drove out to the pathetic trailer park Tim McVeigh called home when he was in Kingman. A Newsweek *reporter was pulling up at the same time, and we worked together to try to interview a bored woman who ran the general store. I noticed bags of horse and dog feed and all kinds of farm equipment, but before I could even frame the question, she snapped, "No, this is* not *where he bought the fertilizer for the bomb. And you're about the sixtieth person to come up with that bright idea."*

I listened half-attentively as she rambled on about her apocalyptic, quasi-Mormon visions of the impending end of the world, to be announced by trumpets and acts of senseless violence like the Oklahoma City bombing. The only useful bit of information she gave us was to talk to the trailer park manager, who was exercising his horses back at the corral.

Canyon West Trailer Park owner Bob Regin looked tired and wrung out. No surprise, since he had gone over the same ground for every cop and major media outlet west of the Mississippi by the time we got to him. Regin said McVeigh was a total loner who was just looking for a place to fit in. He rented trailer #11 in June of 1993 and also rented a post office box at the Mail Room in Kingman.

"Tim was a real loner who never drank, or dated, or even had any friends over," Regin said. "I almost felt sorry for him, because it was like he didn't have any kind of life at all. He would just go to work, come home, sleep, get up, go to work, and come home. He struck me as a guy who was trying to figure out what he was going to do with his life. I guess he made some bad choices. The only things that might have been signs were that he had rifles stacked in the corners of his trailer. I also used to see him on the weekends wearing camouflage clothing. But that's not unusual.

A lot of people around here wear army fatigues, because they're so comfortable and cheap.

"When he came to me and said he was moving out, I was sorry to see him go. He said, 'I just can't find steady work around here.' I said, 'I can lower your rent until you get back on your feet.' I was that eager to keep him because he was such a good tenant. He was paying $250 a month. But he just said, 'No, I'll go someplace else.' "

The interview was cut short when a couple of FBI agents, dressed in shorts and Hawaiian shirts, but sporting web belts festooned with radios and 9 mms, walked up behind Regin, grabbed him by the back of the neck, and began to frog-march him toward a shed. "Interview over," one of them shot back over his shoulder.

I went in search of McVeigh's neighbors. I found the only black man I had seen in Kingman, who had a real up-close-and-personal sense of what it was like to live in a community of violent, well-armed loners who despised him solely because of his race.

"You could tell that he had been in the Army," Jason Jatho began. "He carried himself differently, was more aware of his surroundings. He never had anyone over at his house. Ever. It was actually kinda' sad. He must have been lonely. But there are a lot of weird things that go on around here. There are militias all over the place, and a lot of racism around here.

"There used to be a sign on a house down the road that said something like 'Better not be any black people around here after dark.' And when I go out jogging, guys in pickup trucks will drive by and scream 'Nigger!' at me. Straight up, it freaks me out that I lived next to somebody who did this."

After McVeigh left the trailer park and quit his job as a security guard for State Security, he got a job in the lumber department of True Value Hardware in February 1994. Workers at True Value were intimidated by the FBI, who told them not to talk to the press, and McVeigh's new address was also being kept under wraps.

However, it was at True Value that I ran into Willis, an emaciated, pimply-faced skinhead who claimed to have been a friend of McVeigh and who offered to be my guide.

"I can take you out to where the training camps and bomb-manufacturing plants are," Willis promised. "We've been training for this day for years. If the Feds try to come in there, we'll shoot them full of holes. There are caves and provisions and mine fields and machine guns."

"We?" I asked. "What the hell are you doing here, then? Shouldn't you be out digging a tank trap or cleaning a rifle or something?"

I was beginning to notice that Willis had some strange tics, and that his bloodshot eyes tended to wander. His arms were scabby and, to put it as delicately as I can, he could have used a touch of Right Guard.

"Uhhh, well, I useta be in there with them. But they . . . they got too extreme. They wanted me to go out and kill niggers and spics, but I said no. I'm not like that. I just think that, uh, white people shouldn't get pushed around. You know? Live and let live," he said uneasily, shifting his weight from foot to foot.

I got the distinct impression that Willis wasn't kicked out on moral grounds, but because the little ferret was so hooked on crank that he was useless, even to a bunch as skeevy as the neo-Nazis.

I decided to take him up on his offer anyway. I gave him some money for gas, and we headed out into the desert east of town. Willis kept up a running monologue about how the place he was taking me had been used by various groups as a training site to teach young antigovernment rebels how to kill silently, how to shoot machine guns accurately (which is more difficult than you would think), and how to fabricate and plant explosives.

Willis kept forgetting which cactus he had to turn at and had to keep slamming on the brakes, jumping out, and crawling on the roof of the pickup to get his bearings. Finally we got to a cluster of shacks that had been recently torched and burned down to stubs of timber. Sifting through the ashes, I found spent 9 mm cartridges, but considering the locale, I probably could have found them in the dirt outside just about anyone's house.

"They musta burned the place down," Willis tried to explain. "To destroy the evidence. See, over there is where they would make us crawl through the brush. And that hole there? That's where they tested some of the new plastique stuff. If Tim had used that in Oklahoma City, he would have taken out the whole downtown. We got big plans. Got a chemist come in, and he's going to make nerve gas. So when the Feds shoot tear gas at us, we'll shoot nerve gas right back at them."

He babbled on. "And then there's the Big Plan. We're gonna recruit somebody to work in a nuclear reactor or missile silo, and take a little bit of stuff each day until we got enough to make our own nuke. And then we're going to set it off in Washington. Take out the whole city. Start over from scratch and do things right."

As plans go, I certainly couldn't accuse them of thinking small, although most of it sounded like complete bullshit to me. Then again, a week earlier, the idea of a misfit like McVeigh pulling off the Oklahoma City bombing would have made me laugh.

I told Willis that this wasn't good enough, that he had to take me someplace where there were actual people around that I could interview. "For all I know, this is where your grandma lived until she started smoking in bed," I taunted.

Willis gulped and looked away, thinking. Then he said, "I think I know where everyone moved to, way out in the high desert. A couple hours' drive, at least, even from here. I'll take you there, but once we get there, you're on your own. I'll just drop you off, because they don't like strangers and I don't want them knowing I showed you where they are."

Somehow the thought of walking unannounced and un-escorted into the compound of a group that in the best of times was violent and paranoid and now had real reason to slip their leashes didn't sound all that attractive.

"No fucking way," I told Willis. "I'm paying you to be my guide. You're coming with me, to tell them it's okay to talk to me, that I'm not trying to set them up."

Willis looked ready to abandon me on the spot until I pulled out $300 and waved it in his face.

Off we went. Here's a useful tip I picked up along the way: Never let a speed freak drive cross-country when it's been hours since he fixed up and he's freaking out about a possible confrontation with his former skinhead buddies.

Willis seemed to be having real trouble concentrating. The truck kept weaving off the nominal trails and bouncing painfully over hummocks and dry streambeds. We rounded a stand of sagebrush and almost ran into a canyon wall. Willis wrenched the wheel and set off at a right angle. In a few minutes we almost ran into another canyon wall. And then another. And another. Somehow Willis had managed to run us into a box canyon and didn't find his way out.

Then things got even more pleasant. Willis was flooring it, frantically trying to get out, when the truck came over a rise and jammed itself onto a huge boulder. BAM! The wheels spun in the sand, and the truck refused to budge.

Willis was making chicken noises and bouncing his fore-head off the dashboard. I reached over and shut off the engine.

"I can't believe you just did that," I said. "I thought you said you knew this desert."

"Yeah, well, not this part. What do we do now?"

"Well, unless you want to walk back, I suggest you get off your ass and help me push your truck off the rock."

The truck was wedged too tight, although fate was smil-ing on us a little bit: The oil pan was still attached, and the axle wasn't snapped. Willis was casting longing glances at his glovebox—no doubt where his stash was hidden. Before *he could get loaded again, I grabbed him and forced him to come with me to start uprooting thorns and shrubs and bushes to stuff under the wheels to provide traction. Then we had to take a couple of planks and try to shovel away the heaps of sand that had been kicked up by the spinning wheels.*

It was boiling hot, and it took hours. We ran out of water right at the end, when we had to brace ourselves against the rock and heave while the truck was in reverse. Suddenly the truck broke free and was rolling wildly away from us. We chased it, screeching, until it smacked into a cactus and slowed down enough for Willis to jump in and slam on the brakes.

I arrived back at the hotel frayed and ready to snap. The FBI men saw my dirty, ripped, disheveled clothing and smirked.

I didn't discover the real reason why for six more months.

One day in October, I looked into my mailbox in the Star *office and discovered an official envelope from the Justice Department, U.S. Attorney, Western District. Wondering what I had run afoul of this time, I opened it up and freaked–out.*

The letter was an official notice that they had tapped my phone lines while I was in Kingman. "Pursuant to court order blah blah blah, an electronic intercept was placed on your phone lines blah blah, conversations were monitored." I guess the Feds have to tell people their lines have been tapped six months after they've done it. As near as I could deduce, either my lines were tapped because I had been hanging around Willis and they wanted to know if I was associated with some radical movement, or they just wanted to see if I was coming up with something they weren't.

I just hoped they had had fun listening to me rail at the accountants over my expenses.

11

MORBID CURIOSITY

Brentwood, California
June 1994

I had scarcely walked into the Star office when I was quickly dispatched to an address only blocks from where Lysa and I lived. The details were sketchy at best: Bob said he thought there had been a couple of murders outside O.J. Simpson's house. We didn't know yet if his ex-wife was involved.

At about nine-forty in the morning, I arrived at the now-famous townhouse on Bundy to see a traffic jam of police cars and TV trucks. More camera crews were hustling in from every direction, carrying tripods and boom mikes. A pair of grim-looking detectives quietly slipped across the street in front of me and started going from house to house. A big white coroner's truck was parked in front of the townhouse and forensics specialists were loading two gurneys with sheeted and strapped-down bodies into the back. I tried to walk up to a couple of lounging cops to ask *questions and was immediately told that the media and public were confined to the other side of the street. I walked over to where TV crews were interviewing neighbors who were just as intently questioning them.*

Nobody knew anything.

Another Star *reporter, the excitable Jennifer Bialow, was also there trying to talk to neighbors who were more interested in getting in front of TV cameras so they could see themselves on the five o'clock news.*

Eventually a carefully coifed, well-dressed detective sauntered across the street in the general direction of the densest concentration of TV cameras. It was like waving a juicy steak in front of a kennel full of starving dogs. All the camera crews and reporters immediately shoved for position, forming a semicircle. The cop, Lt. John Rogers, looked more like a Hollywood leading man than a grizzled street veteran, but there was a no-nonsense look about him, and in his eyes burned a fierce intelligence.

He started giving us enough tiny tidbits to keep us from charging across the street, cameras rolling. Yes, this was the house of Nicole Simpson. Yes, she was one of the victims.

I asked if there were any signs of a robbery. Rogers seemed to consider a second. "No, no signs of a robbery, nothing was taken. No forced entry."

Right away I knew this was not going to be run-of-the-mill.

Rogers kept answering questions. Nicole's two children were in the house when the murders happened. No, they were not harmed. No, they didn't wake up, they were still sleeping when police arrived. As yet there were no witnesses and no suspects.

The more Rogers talked, the more I felt a kind of tension building. After you do a lot of interviews with people who have things to hide, you start noticing signs that they have something they want to tell you but can't make up their minds if they should.

Then, out of nowhere, Rogers volunteered some information: "We have been to O.J. Simpson's house, and he is not there. He is out of town." He looked around, gauging the expressions on the reporters around him.

I asked, "Why did you go to O.J.'s house if he was out of town?"

Rogers paused, then looked me right in the eye. You could see wheels turning in his head, scales tipping to and fro. Then a calmness settled over him as he reached a decision. And lied to me. "We just wanted to see if he was okay."

He continued to look at me steadily, trying to see my reaction. It was a patent understatement, the kind that reveals as much as it conceals. On the surface, it can't be pointed out as a lie later because it's plausible enough, but he knew that we knew that there could be only one reason cops were sent to O.J.'s house.

They suspected O.J. did it.

Rogers left that hanging in the air and walked back across the street.

It was a masterful way of telling those of us who could read between the lines that they considered O.J. a suspect.

I grabbed Bialow by the arm and walked her a few yards down the sidewalk. "What was that all about?" she asked blankly.

"Give me the cell phone. I gotta' call Bob. They suspect O.J."

"Where did you come up with that? They said he was out of town."

"Just gimme the phone."

I made the call and was told by Bob to come back to the office. I wanted to hang out and get more from the neighbors, but Bob had a couple of other stories that were demanding attention. Within a minute of getting back to the office, I was sent right back out to the West L.A. police station, because by that time O.J. had been arrested. Bob wanted me there with my camera when they dragged O.J. out of the police car and into the holding tank.

When I got to the police station, all the TV crews had already arrived, some of them claiming that Channel 9 had gotten footage of O.J. being handcuffed at his house. I went into the station and saw a pretty blond producer trying to charm the desk sergeants into telling her whether or not O.J. was in the building. Doug Bruckner of "Hard Copy" was on two phones at once next to the soda machines, trying to convince whoever was on the other end that O.J. really had been arrested. A patrolman had a photographer by the lapels and was lecturing him on why it's not a good idea to try to jump over the desk and run around the squad room to get a picture. A couple other paparazzi were poking their heads around the corner and giggling at their busted comrade. It was the old familiar media circus.

The producer finally convinced one of the bemused desk officers to go back and bug the detectives. He reappeared a minute later looking chastened and serious, and told us that they would neither confirm nor deny O.J.'s presence in the station.

Which we naturally took as a confirmation, since after all, if he wasn't there, then why bother being cute about it?

As it turned out, O.J. actually was not on the premises but at police headquarters downtown, foolishly refusing to have his lawyer present while he answered questions for hours.

Photographer Alan Zanger arrived in his new truck and immediately started bragging about how Michelle Pfeiffer had "bought" him the truck because he had just made $50,000 on a picture of her. Zanger is famous for staying on a stakeout twenty hours straight, eating, drinking, and pissing in his truck. I've seen him do it while driving. He pins the steering wheel with his knees, unzips and stuffs himself into an empty Evian bottle, and lets fly. All this while driving a stick shift and talking on a cell phone at the same time. When he's finished, he tosses the bottle out the *window into traffic. On a purely physical level, it's an amazing display of coordination. Disgusting, but amazing.*

I got paged. I called in and was told to return to the office again. I was sent to Nicole's brother's house down in Long Beach.

Rolf Baur lives in one of the less desirable areas of that increasingly depressed city. Half the neighborhood was out on their front stoops, drinking out of wrinkled paper bags. The other half lounged squinting under Raider caps on street corners shaking hands a lot and passing back and forth tiny glass vials.

Rolf's wife talked to me through the screen door while holding two screaming infants. She said that Rolf wasn't there, that he learned about his sister's murder that morning by phone, that he was very upset. She said that they had often spent time with O.J. at family barbecues, that her kids had played with his kids, and that he had always been nice to them. She said she was worried about Nicole's kids and how they would have to deal with not having a mother anymore.

I asked her if she had talked to any other reporters yet, and she said no, but this lady from Channel 5 had called her about sixty times, and so she stopped answering the phone.

This was the last time I was to talk to her, but she later became a real key to the tabloid coverage of the case. An Enquirer *reporter named Allan Butterfield, who spoke Spanish, was assigned to hound and shadow Rolf and his wife until they cracked. They then became the* Enquirer's *pipeline to the Brown family and would tell them in advance when Nicole's kids were going to visit the gravesite, describe the family's agony, leak modeling pictures of Nicole, and so on.*

The next day was the Star's *deadline, and I worked with five other reporters to throw together a story about the murders and get it past the lawyers and into the issue. Already I could tell this was going to be a story that was going* to hang around for a while because of all the TV attention it was getting.

Bob sent me to Laguna Beach to find where Nicole's parents lived and try to get an interview with them. All we knew was that they lived somewhere called Monarch Bay, which didn't seem to be on any map. So I got on Pacific Coast Highway in Laguna and started driving around, asking questions. After about three tries, I got a surfer to point it out on a map and drove to the gated community. I knew it was the place because of the knot of frustrated photographers on the sidewalk out in front. I pulled in and the frumpy matron in the guard shack immediately went off at me, yelling, "You try and run in there like that fella from the Enquirer and I'll call the cops and have them arrest your ass. I'm getting sick of all you people. Why don't you go home and leave them alone?"

I drove to a pay phone, called Bob, and said, "There's no way to get in." He told me to start looking around for people who knew Nicole or the family. That proved to be fruitless.

Thursday was Nicole's funeral, and I was sent to the chapel in Brentwood where the service was being held. It was another mob scene, with about three hundred reporters, photographers, and TV weasels packed in across the street from the entrance, skirmishing with cops and hired security guards and screaming questions at the mourners as they emerged from their cars and went into the church. At first, I had thought about infiltrating the services. It's easy if you're dressed in black and keep your head down and don't talk to anyone. But I saw that as people went in, everyone's name was getting checked off on a list.

It really didn't matter anyway, because five minutes after I got there, Bob called and told me to go to the cemetery where Nicole was going to be buried. In Orange County. About fifty miles away.

"Okay, where is this place?" I asked.

"Aaaah, I don't know. Somewhere near the family's home," Bob said.

"Well, what's the name of it?"

"Aaah, it was in the paper this morning. I can't remember it off the top of my head."

"How am I supposed to get there?"

"Ask one of the other reporters. Maybe they know."

I started heading south toward Orange County, flipping through the Los Angeles Times while I was driving, looking for the name of the cemetery. I found it, called information on my cell phone, got the address, then called another reporter in the office and had them give me directions.

It wasn't hard to figure out when I was getting close; TV vans were all over the place. I pulled onto the gravel shoulder and joined ten AP and LA Times photographers who were staring over a fence. We were about five hundred yards away, a long shot for even the most powerful camera lens. I pulled out my binoculars and camera and started studying the terrain, looking for easy approaches and places to hide. It looked pretty bleak. There was a steep, brushy gully and a high fence between us and the area where all the wreaths and the podium were set up, and the sheriffs were out in force, walking the perimeter. Even if I could make it across a wide-open field to the tree line, I'd still be two hundred and fifty yards from the action, with nothing but sloping cemetery in front of me. I'd be shooting uphill, through brush, with almost certain arrest and film confiscation if the deputies heard my camera go off.

I decided to stay put and let the guys getting the $250 day rates go for the killer shots.

It was a thirty-minute wait for the funeral procession, where all the photographers lined the street and tried to shoot grieving relatives and friends through moving windshields. I concentrated on the entrance, where O.J. was out and moving around. I could see people smile to his face and immediately turn and whisper to one another behind his back. I focused on his face and saw no signs of tears or grief when he approached kids and family.

It was all very strange. I wondered if anyone could be cold-blooded enough to show up at the funeral of someone they had killed, acting like nothing was wrong. You would have to be pathologically disconnected from your emotions to be able to carry it off. I saw Nicole's sisters sobbing as her coffin was unloaded and carried to the open grave.

The photographers started shooting away as the mourners gathered in a circle under an awning designed to shield them from hovering helicopters. A fat, sweaty "sidewalk photographer" with battered, junky equipment rushed up and started whining. In the hierarchy of paparazzi, the sidewalk photographer is equivalent to festering swamp slime; their job is to stand on the sidewalk outside trendy clubs and restaurants to take pictures of the celebs. As a rule, they aren't very intelligent, because all they have to do is stand and shoot whatever walks in front of them. In real news situations like this, they flounder.

Peering through his tiny lens, the newcomer realized he wasn't going to get anything usable from that distance. His eyes bugged out and he started whimpering like a four-year-old who can't see the circus: "Hey, guys! Hey, guys! Can someone loan me a lens? I can't see what's going on." The others stolidly ignored him.

"Fine, then, be that way," he sniffed, hauling his bulk over the barbed-wire fence and trudging down the hill to the cemetery border, trailed by a gaggle of wide-eyed local teens. About ten minutes later he came puffing up the hill, red-faced from a severe tongue-lashing at the hands of an irate deputy.

Meanwhile, I noticed that two young children had slipped between the legs of the black-clad grownups circling Nicole's coffin and were running around and playing on the sloping lawn. I looked closer and realized it was Nicole's kids. Laughing and shrieking, oblivious to the somber surroundings, they were acting like regular kids trapped in a dull grownup affair. The symbolism and irony of that, of life and innocence very visibly going on in the midst of death, darkness, and guilt, made me queasy, so I loaded up my truck and left.

On the Friday of the infamous low-speed chase, I had been assigned to drive, for the third straight day, down to Laguna to scare up someone who was a close friend of Nicole's who would talk to the Star on the record about her terrible marriage. And I was to see if they had any pictures, too.

We had little idea who Nicole's friends in the area were, and when I had called some of them on the phone earlier, they were exasperated over the hundreds of other calls they had gotten and would give only vague generalities about what a nice mother Nicole was to her kids. I decided to go to a location where I knew they had photos and knew something about Nicole: Laguna Beach High School. I ran into a teacher there who was a friend of Nicole's sister Denise, and who let me photograph the ycarbook pictures of Nicole on the homecoming float. She directed me to a restaurant where the teachers were having an end-of-the-year lunch, and told me who to talk to. I went there, saw them all, and decided to let them finish their meal before barging in and giving them the third degree. While I was lounging around, I talked with a chef who told me he had once dated Nicole's sister Tanya.

I could hardly believe my luck. I started pumping him for details about O.J. and Nicole, and he told me how Tanya had to be their babysitter and how the family tiptoed around the subject of O.J. abusing Nicole.

Then he casually dropped a bombshell. "Yeah, wc were listening to the radio in the back. The cops went to arrest O.J. and he took off."

Immediately, I could see the next day's headline in my head, and I blurted it out: "The Juice is Loose!"

The teachers later blew me off because they were sick of answering questions about Nicole, but at that point I didn't care. I walked back to my car with my mind in a whirl. I could see this story leaping onto a whole new level of prominence. A millionaire celebrity on the run from charges that he slaughtered two people, one of whom was his ex-wife.

It doesn't get much more sensational than this, I thought.

With O.J. on the run, we were going to get tons of cold calls from people claiming to have seen him. The police manhunt was going to be beyond intense, because the LAPD would be crucified for letting him get away. And if he did manage to remain at large for more than a few days, magazines and newspapers would start sending reporters all over the world to Tijuana, Rio de Janeiro, Tahiti, anyplace O.J. might be hiding out from extradition. A lot of people were going to get expensive vacations on the company.

I phoned the office and was told to go talk to the Orange County sheriffs to see what they were going to do. While pulling into the parking lot, I heard attorneys Robert Shapiro and Robert Kardashian get on the radio and read O.J.'s handwritten note. It sounded just like a suicide note. Just when it seemed the story couldn't get any wilder, it took another lurch over the line toward complete surreality.

Little did I know how much farther the situation had to go.

The cops were too busy to talk to me at that point, so I went to the Brown family compound to see if anyone there was going to give a statement. About twenty other reporters had had the same idea, and a milling mass of them stood on the sidewalk trying to cajole the security guards to let them in.

I got paged and was told that everyone had rushed to Nicole's house, because O.J. had supposedly called in and said he was going to kill himself there. I called Lysa at home and told her to get over there. Meanwhile, I headed back to see the sheriffs. On the way, I got another call from

Bob telling me to go to the cemetery. O.J. hadn't shown up at Nicole's house, and he might be headed down this way.

At the cemetery, a bunch of deputies were standing by their cars in the parking lot, listening to the police radio. Suddenly, they all ran for their cars and peeled rubber. I figured they must be on to something, so I gave chase.

The next thing I knew, I was on the I–5 heading north, about a half mile behind fifteen or twenty sheriff's cruisers. A helicopter was hovering overhead. I figured they must have O.J. cornered somewhere and there was going to be a big standoff, maybe even a gun battle.

I tuned the radio to the news station. The first thing I heard was a continuing bulletin about how Orange County sheriffs were chasing O..J. north on the I–5. He was in the back of his white Ford Bronco, holding a gun to his chest, and his pal Al Cowlings was at the wheel.

I looked up. Way ahead of the sheriffs was a lone white Bronco. "This is too weird," I said.

The whole procession kept slowing down and speeding up, and TV vans and photographers started joining the pack. A formation of cop cars broke off the main pack and dropped back to keep us at a distance, because some of the photographers were weaving at eighty miles an hour, trying to get close enough to take a picture. The chariot races of Ben-Hur *had nothing on us.*

I called Bob. "You'll never believe where I am," I said.

"Hold on, I'm watching O.J. get chased. He's on the five heading north. They say he just wants to go to his mother's house."

"I know. I'm behind him."

"Jesus Christ! Can you see him?"

"Naaah, he's too far away. The cops won't let us get close."

"Well, stick with it. Take a picture if you can, and call me."

The chase was the first event of the O.J. mania. All his

friends and fans started calling up the radio show and begging O.J. to pull over.

By the time we got near his mother's house off the 91 freeway, thousands of looky-loo's had turned out to line the freeway, holding signs that said GO JUICE GO, standing and cheering, waving at the camera, yelling "Hi, Mom!" and giving the number one sign.

Traffic in the opposite direction had totally stopped as everyone pulled over and lined the freeway divider to gawk. Young guys wearing Raider hats darted in and out of traffic, trying to get close enough for a look. There were fifty near-misses every minute as the TV vans cut each other off and jockeyed for position. The overpasses were filled with people aiming video cameras, mothers holding their children up to see the parade, self-appointed media critics spitting on our windshields.

I called my mom in Wisconsin; she, too, was watching the chase. "Take a picture so I can prove to the neighbors that you were there," she ordered.

All the while I was having this conversation, I was trying to steer, shift gears, hold the phone, keep the stubborn power cord in the cigarette lighter, hold my Canon steady, and try to focus on O.J. through my grimy windshield. Unfortunately, performing these tasks requires at least five hands. My steering became a little erratic and I almost side-swiped a cop. The next thing I knew, one of the cops had pulled behind me and was waving me over.

"That's it! You're sitting this one out," he yelled.

I could only watch as the whole cavalcade continued north without me. Bringing up the rear were a couple of vanloads of hooting frat boys, sticking their Polaroids out the window and absurdly waving USC banners in a twisted display of school spirit.

"I can't take this anymore," I mumbled and headed home, exhausted and drained. When I got there, I turned on the TV and walked out on my balcony to watch twenty

*helicopters buzz overhead only a couple miles away as O.J.
finally gave himself up and was taken to jail.*

*The next few weeks were the start of a giant fishing expe-
dition, where every reporter was thrown headlong into the
Simpsons' private life as we all tried to figure out how and
why O.J. had done it. At the time, all we had were sketchy
details of the murders, O.J.'s arrest in 1989 for beating Nicole, and guesswork. Facts and details were bandied about
in the first flush of discovery—blood on the driveway,
bloody gloves at O.J.'s house, a shovel and plastic wrap in
the back of the Bronco—but the only figure of any signifi-
cance was, and is, ninety-five million. As in, more than
ninety-five million people tuned in to the freeway chase.
That translates into a very simple equation: lots of people
watching = lots of advertisers = lots of money.*

*All the local TV stations and the TV tabloid shows were
in complete meltdown. They threw every person they had
into the story, and the pressure on them to come up with an
exclusive was intense enough to turn coal into diamonds.
Unfortunately, most of the gems they purported to uncover
turned out to be fool's gold. It was reported that cops had
found a bloody ski mask at the scene, that O.J. had stolen a
huge Rambo-style knife with a serrated edge that matched
the wounds, that O.J. had castrated Ron Goldman before
he died, that Ron and Nicole were lovers.*

*Meanwhile, every nutcase on the West Coast who had
slipped off his or her antipsychotic meds called the Star,
trying to sell a story for a million dollars. They all wanted
the money up front before they talked, and said they feared
for their lives because they knew the real story.*

*"What do you think we are, your personal ATM?" I
asked one loony who was demanding $300,000 for an ex-
clusive telepathic interview with Kato the dog.*

*The prevailing theories seemed to be: O.J. hadn't com-
mitted the murders but knew who did; it was the Mob, as
payback for O.J.'s gambling debts in Vegas, and if O.J. told,
they would kill the rest of his family; his son Jason did it*

and O.J. was just covering up for him; Colombians had done it to collect on drug debts; Nicole was a high-priced call girl, O.J. was her pimp, and she was killed by a rival.

But a couple of people did have truthful, legitimate stories to tell. The attention quickly focused on limo driver Allan Park and two guys who said they had seen O.J. buy a knife while working on the Naked Gun set.

I was assigned to try to make a deal for either one of these two stories, but what happened in both is a classic example of the pitfalls of tabloid journalism.

A movie crewman named Scott Moody was acting as the "agent" to sell the story about O.J. buying the knife. This is common, because most people think the tabs are going to somehow find out who they are, kidnap them, and sweat the story out of them in some downtown warehouse under the glare of a bare lightbulb. They called the Star second, as usual, to check out if the price they had been quoted from the National Enquirer was fair.

"They're going to pay us twenty-five thousand for the story, but if you can come up with more money, you can have it," Moody told me. "Hey, we don't care, whoever's the highest bidder."

I went to Bob. He had to call New York before we could make a move. They dithered and finally said, "Offer him five thousand."

Huh?

Why would anyone sign up with us for a $20,000 loss? I was ashamed even to make the phone call.

As it turns out, it would have been smarter for them to sign the contract with us. Because in every contract, there is a clause that basically says, "If we get the same story from someone else, we can run that and not have to pay you a dime."

The Enquirer sat the two neophytes down and interviewed them for hours, wringing out every detail: which knife shop it was, where it was located, and so on. They then went to that knife shop and asked to speak to the clerks who sold O.J. the stiletto knife. They got the clerks and the owners to go on the record for $12,000.

Much better sources. Much better story. And the two poor saps got exactly nada.

A week later, I got a call from Moody. "Uh, we got your message. We'll tell you our story for seventy-five hundred," he said hopefully.

I told him to tell his story to the D.A. and hung up.

At the same time, I was being sent to Allan Park's house, which I found to have a complete media siege force encamped out front, and then to the house of his boss, where the infamous limo was sticking out of the garage.

"Can you see any blood on it? Is there any way you could get inside it?" I was asked. Not wanting either a grand theft auto rap or tampering with evidence charge brought against me, I said I thought the car had an alarm and was under surveillance.

Later that summer, I was to interview Park's former employer, who said that he had fired Alan for being chronically late and irresponsible. He wanted $5,000 for the story, which would have undermined the credibility of Park, who was a key witness in testifying that O.J. was not in his house at the time of the murders. However, at the time, the tabloids were far more interested in coming up with anything that seemed to prove O.J. had done it.

Unfortunately, in their rush to get an exclusive, the tabloids tarnished and made useless a witness who was able to place O.J. near the scene of the murders at about the time they took place. Jill Shively said that she saw O.J. in his white Bronco, driving like a maniac, panicked and beeping his horn, blocking traffic at the intersection of Bundy and San Vicente. This is the kind of testimony that usually results in defendants choking to death on peach-flavored gas in the green room in San Quentin.

What followed has resulted in a change in the California state law regarding witnesses to crimes. Jill made a deal with the Star and "Hard Copy" to tell her story about *seeing O.J. that night. The* Star *paid her about $5,000 for the interview, but it was a real high-wire-without-a-net affair. Because of the gag order imposed on witnesses after they testified before the Grand Jury (remember, in the early days, the D.A.s put Simpson in front of a Grand Jury to indict him so they could legally close the hearings and not have to deal with the media crush), the* Star *had to scramble to get the contract executed and interview Shively before she was called as a witness. It may not have broken the letter of the law, but it sure as hell broke the spirit.*

When it came out in her testimony that she had been paid by the tabloids to say that O.J. was speeding away from the scene in his car, it totally destroyed her credibility as a witness. To admit under cross-examination that your testimony is for sale to the highest bidder makes a witness look like she's fabricating everything to make a quick buck.

The Los Angeles District Attorney's office was rather annoyed with us after that.

Meanwhile, all the stories about O.J. and Nicole and the wife-beating were starting to surface. We were getting dozens of calls a day from would-be sources who purported to have eyewitnessed savage scenes of abuse and humiliation, as well as hundreds of women who claimed to have had affairs with O.J. while he was married to Nicole.

But it was at the end of summer that I unexpectedly got to see what it was like when that immense microscope of international scrutiny was trained on me and a story I was working on.

It started innocently enough. A freelancer called in to say he had a story about a "porn starlet who was pregnant with the baby of baseball's highest-paid player." Since housewives really aren't that keen on sports figures no matter what they do, I shrugged and made a mental note to pitch the idea. Then the freelancer said that the starlet had been Al Cowlings's girlfriend and that Al had revealed to her that O.J. had confessed to him about committing the murders.

Boing.

Climbing back into my chair, I tried to tell him calmly that we might be interested in such an interview, if the girl had any proof of what she was saying, and who she was. I hung up the phone, called the news editor, and was told "Get that girl! Promise her anything!"

For the next two weeks, my life was turned upside down as I "babysat" a dark-haired sex pistol named Jennifer Peace (a.k.a. Devon Shire), her dog Katie, and a parade of ex-porn starlets at luxury hotels. I escorted her everywhere, soothed her nerves before she went to testify before the Grand Jury on Al Cowlings, and was deluged with phone calls from every TV show, newspaper, and magazine on the West Coast.

It's become an axiom of mine: The bigger the story, the more trouble it is to bring in. This story proved the rule.

I went to Jennifer's tiny house in West Hollywood, gave her a confidentiality agreement (basically promising we wouldn't rip her off), and sat down to discuss what she had to say and what it would take for her to say it to us. She said that she was living under constant harassment, from the media staking out her house to try to interview her to the cops dragging her away in front of her neighbors for real questioning.

Her court subpoena gave us a handy way around a real sticky point in her story: Jennifer didn't have any proof whatsoever that she had ever dated Al Cowlings. No pictures, hotel bills, restaurant receipts, gifts, nothing. But if we could say in our story that "Jennifer told the D.A.s that she was Cowlings's girlfriend," then we could get away with it, because she HAD told them that. Complicating everything was the fallout from the Shively case, which had the entire New York Star *editorial board terrified and sweating that they were going to be dragged away in chains if they tampered with another witness.*

To get the deal done was going to require clear, rational thought and quick and decisive action. Unfortunately, we flip-flopped around on that poor woman more times than Mary Lou Retton's floor exercise, leaving her with a lingering sense of bitterness and betrayal toward the Star.

I got the sketchy outline of the story from Jennifer and phoned in a brief synopsis: Two days after the freeway chase, Al Cowlings had broken down in tears to Jennifer in a Brentwood hotel and admitted to her that O.J. had called him the night of the murders and confessed. She said she had also been present when O.J. had short-circuited and started beating Nicole for snorting the last of the cocaine.

I was elated at landing such a big story, and the editors in Tarrytown already had the headline composed—O.J. TO AL: I DID IT! I was told to take Jennifer to the Four Seasons Hotel in Beverly Hills for the full interview and photo session, and give her a contract for $25,000. She was really starting to freak–out about all the attention she was getting and was more than happy to be able to get out of her house. I picked her up, bought all kinds of stuff for her dog, checked her into a nice room (on my credit card), and sat down to go over the interview on tape and in detail. A couple of hours later, I went to the freelancers' room and said, "I think we have a problem."

The story Jennifer was telling now wasn't quite the same one she had told earlier. For example, Cowlings no longer said that O.J. had confessed to him, just that O.J. had called him up and said, "I've just done something terrible." Which is not the same as admitting to a double murder. I went back up and for another two hours went over and over with Jennifer the testimony she was going to give to the Grand Jury.

The next day, when I told the editors about the hitches and her being subpoenaed, they exploded and ordered me to tell her to get out of the hotel room immediately, that we weren't going to do a story with her. Jennifer was livid.

A day later, the editors had changed their minds. I was ordered to go back to her house and somehow sweet-talk Jennifer into trusting me again, that we wanted to do the *story with her after all and would put her up in any hotel she wanted.*

I searched the area for a hotel that would also take a dog and settled on the chi-chi Ma Maison Sofitel. I immediately started getting whiny phone calls from New York wondering if I could find someplace where the rooms were $15 a night cheaper. Jennifer wasn't helping matters any by bringing all her friends over for free dinners on the Star *and ordering filet mignon for her dog.*

Meanwhile, the palimony suit Jennifer was preparing to file against the baseball player was also causing turmoil, as headcracking private investigator Anthony Pellicano somehow tracked her down. I was staying in the room next door and she ran to get me to listen in to what he was saying. It was a constant stream of threats, flattery, blackmail, and intimidation, all aimed at getting Jennifer to have an abortion and not bear the child in exchange for unnamed but hinted-at considerations.

It was one of the few things about the episode that made me feel better about myself. I may have been skirting the law with a witness to a capital crime, but at least I wasn't trying to bribe a mother into killing her unborn child.

I wrote and filed the story. Soon afterward I started getting phone calls asking me if it would be possible for Jennifer to remember events another way. The headline I'VE DONE SOMETHING TERRIBLE just didn't have the same ring as I DID IT, and they were wondering if there was anything I could do, and if so, how much would it take?

It was my job to figure out how to get them what they wanted. I immediately realized that no matter how things shook out, if I tried to accommodate them, I was going to be the one left without a seat when the music stopped. Either Jennifer would go along and change her testimony to the Grand Jury, committing perjury at my request, or she was going to refuse and tell the D.A.s that I had tried to bribe her to do so. And when the house of cards started collapsing, everyone involved would point fingers at me and brand me a reckless and irresponsible reporter who acted without orders, saving their own asses while leaving me to twist slowly in the wind.

I explained the situation to Jennifer and told her to stick to her guns and tell only the absolute truth, no matter what. "The problem is, I've been over this thing so many times that my head is turning to mush. I don't know what's right or wrong anymore, and I'm afraid that I'll say something wrong and then they'll throw me in jail and take my baby away from me," Jennifer said, bursting into tears.

She was under so much stress and early-pregnancy hormones that her emotions were raging out of control. She would lose her temper over the phone, screaming and cursing one minute, and then curl up into a ball and talk like an unsure little girl the next.

Lysa was getting suspicious and jealous and gave me a razor-eyed glare every time I was around Jennifer. She interrogated me mercilessly about her. If I made any kind of remark that could be construed as positive, she would accuse me of "lusting" after her. Lysa moved into the Ma Maison with me, ostensibly to help me with the story, but more likely to assuage her paranoia.

Back at my apartment, my answering machine tape overloaded from desperate TV reporters begging me to tell them what Jennifer was saying and offering me big bucks under the table to arrange an interview with her. Somehow word leaked out that we were at the Ma Maison, and camera crews started staking out the lobby. I had to sneak Jennifer out a fire exit into my waiting car, throw a beach towel over her head, and drive like a maniac to get her out of the hotel and off to her Grand Jury grilling.

When we got to the courthouse, a wolfpack of fifty reporters descended on us, shouting and screaming questions. I was wearing a suit and sunglasses and was trying to glower convincingly to make them believe I was her bodyguard.

I had to wait outside the room in the thirteenth-floor

hallway. I noticed the cameramen were panning up and down my body, then zooming in on my crotch. Evidently the rumor had gone around that I was Jennifer's boyfriend, a former co-star from her porn past, and they were trying to see if I had the porn-king endowment. Oh God, don't let my mom see this on the noon news, *I prayed.*

Later, in the courthouse elevator, cameramen tried to cram in to get exclusive shots and comments on the way down, and I caught an NBC guy pointing his lens right down Jennifer's ample cleavage. "Hey, cut that out, you perv," I protested.

I moved her to Shutters on the Beach in Santa Monica to get her away from temptation, because other reporters were trying to entice her to talk. When she didn't, they had to make it up themselves. Then, when their fabrications conflicted, they blamed Jennifer and said that she was changing her story and that she was an opportunistic liar.

But now that the story (or some bastardized version of it) had gotten out, the Star *decided not to pay her $25,000. They tried to chisel her down, nickel and dime every part of it. It was only when her lawyer threatened to sue for triple whatever the contract stated that they backed off and sent out the check they owed her.*

Jennifer later signed a contract with King World to do a one-hour special about her story, for which she was paid close to $100,000.

After all the fuss, though, the issue with Jennifer's story on the cover really didn't sell that much better than other issues. The editors became convinced that the only thing that really sold were stories about how badly O.J. had beaten Nicole, what a beast he was, and what an unhappy victim she was. So week after week, we printed nothing but Nicole pictures on the cover and published wilder and wilder stories about what had happened during their marriage. Sales went up nearly 33 percent.

As the story dragged on and on, I was assigned to the L.A. courthouse to get to know some of the players and get my hands on the jury questionnaire. The aim was to try to figure out who the jurors were so we could get to their families and buy up their inside stories. The Star was exiled to a trailer out behind the abandoned Hall of Justice, damaged in the Pretty Big One of 1994.

"We're trailer trash," I muttered, taking stock of the other reporters exiled to the sun-baked parking lot. The most enduring image of Camp O.J. was the ever-ascending scaffolding erected by the TV networks and news magazines. It started when CNN built a little platform so their news anchors could give hourly updates and analyses with the familiar criminal courts building in the background instead of the wildly gesticulating onlookers hawking T-shirts and "DON'T SQUEEZE THE JUICE" buttons. But the scaffolding blocked everyone else's view of the building, so the other networks simply started trying to outdo one another.

The trailers were a kind of gulag for reporters whose publications didn't have enough pull to get them a seat in the overcrowded, incestuous press room. I was saddled with translating for a gang of puzzled reporters from foreign papers.

After the first week, tensions in the little trailer were running high, as pressure to produce banged head-on with the utter lack of anything to do other than watch TV. A couple of thick-necked Vikings who worked for the Norwegian magazine Dagbladet went out and got stinking drunk, then started singing insulting songs about the Germans from Stern and Der Spiegel, which led to a drunken parking-lot brawl.

Every time I would venture into the courthouse proper, the other journalists would react to my presence like piranhas to a porterhouse. I couldn't walk down a hallway without being pulled aside by a cajoling reporter, begging me to let them in on next week's cover story.

"Hey, whatcha' working on? Anything big? What's the latest on (fill in name of Simpson case player here)? Listen, *maybe we could help each other out. Give me a call some-time, and we'll hook up.''*

Within days, I had a stack of business cards. Every Mon-day morning, they'd be poring over the fresh issues of Star, Enquirer, *and* Globe, *scanning for anything they could use to plug into their courthouse updates.*

The other stories that were coming out made sleepy little Brentwood sound like a veritable Sodom and Gomorrah— kinky three-way sex, weeklong drug parties, coke whores, and rampant infidelity. I interviewed a self-described "drug dealer to the stars" who said he had been Faye Resnick's pimp and had tales about O.J. trying to score drugs from him.

The more the trial dragged on, the more we started hav-ing to recycle stories or pull out old stories that hadn't been worth doing when there was so much fresh and juicy mate-rial around. And then there were all the wackos who came and went and got their fifteen minutes of fame. Like Rosa Lopez.

Rosa had talked to a Star *reporter the day of the killings and told him a slew of different stories. First she said O.J. hadn't done it, and he was a real nice guy. Then she said Nicole was mean to the maid and slapped her. Then she said Nicole had chased the maid over to Rosa's house with a knife. Then she said O.J. had chased the maid with a knife, but Rosa had defended the maid. Then she said O.J. had beaten Nicole to a pulp, and a naked Nicole had run across the street to seek shelter in Rosa's arms, chased by a maddened, knife-wielding O.J., but brave Rosa had scared him off, and how much would we pay her for that story, please?*

This woman was supposed to be the defense's star wit-ness. Unbeknownst to me, the Star *swore to the D.A.s that we had never talked to Rosa. I mentioned to some of the reporters down at the courthouse that we had indeed talked to her and found her to be unreliable. A day later, my phone rang.*

It was Christopher Darden.

He wanted to know what we knew about Rosa. I told him what I knew and he seemed pleased, and eager to meet with me. I asked him if Rosa was going to be ordered to stay in the United States to testify, because I had been given a plane ticket to El Salvador and told to follow her there if she fled. He said he wasn't sure, but he didn't think she would be going anywhere soon.

When I told the Star *what Darden had said, the shit hit the fan again. The mildest reaction was, "Tell that fucking LaFontaine to keep his fucking mouth shut!"*

During the trial, I also worked on other celebrity stories. At one point I was negotiating to do an interview with Rick James in Folsom Prison. James said he had all kinds of nasty stories about what O.J. was like when the two of them partied in the 1970s in Buffalo and in the 1980s in L.A. But the interview fell through when the Simpson jury unexpectedly came to a verdict within hours of retiring for deliberations. I was sure that meant they had voted to convict, because an acquittal would have required hours of arm twisting.

I drove Annette Witheridge, a British reporter from the New York office, to the courthouse to report on the scene. An ugly, restless crowd had formed in front of the criminal courts building, and the street had been barricaded off while cops on horseback tried to maintain some semblance of order. The atmosphere was so tense that if two guys had started throwing punches in the crowd, in seconds there would have been a full-fledged riot.

Los Angeles was one giant powderkeg, and I was standing at ground zero. The tension built as the jury filed in, and I saw the cops loosening their clubs and smart photographers wisely strapping their gear to their backs for a quick getaway. Everyone leaned in to listen to the portable radios and Watchmans in the crowd. The verdict was read: not guilty.

Immediately the crowd whooped with joy. A couple of

young black men started jumping up and down in front of me and then turned and gave me the finger, shoving it in my face again and again, screaming, "Fuck you, white boy! Fuck you, you white motherfucker! Fuck you! Ha-ha-ha-ha-ha!"

I was stunned and confused, not just by the verdicts, but by the reaction. What the hell do I have to do with anything? *I wondered.*

Then the families came out of the courthouse sobbing, and the jeers and derision crescendocd again. I heard a white reporter next to me mutter, "Maybe Fuhrman was right about all of them. Pile 'em up and set 'em on fire."

I felt like I was watching the first shots of the next civil war. I wandered back to the trailer feeling sick and defeated, only to be ordered out to a photo lab in the Pacific Palisades.

It wasn't over yet. The Star *had struck a deal with O.J. to get exclusive rights to photos of what he did when he came home. The price was supposed to be top secret, but the number $500,000 leaked out, as well as details of a deal that would allow us to get three more weeks of exclusives out of O.J. for an additional $500,000 a pop.*

The Star *wanted me to help guard the film and make sure that no other paparazzi tried to strong-arm the pictures away from us while we were transporting them from the lab to O.J.'s house, where O.J. and a photographer would go over the prints, choosing which ones they would allow us to use and which ones were too sensitive or damaging to O.J.'s reputation.*

I couldn't believe it. After almost a year and a half of printing stories purporting to show how O.J. was one of the vilest, most evil men on the face of the earth, we were uncritically presenting his side of the story. Not only that, we were allowing him and his advisers to tell us exactly what we were going to say and write about him. We might as well have put up a big sign outside the office designating us as "O.J.'s Official Mouthpiece."

I only brought it up once, asking another reporter, "Don't you think this might backfire on us? A lot of people are going to be really mad at us for taking O.J.'s side and paying him money."

I was told, "Some people might be a little sore, but we're getting the story and the pictures that everyone else would kill to be getting right now."

A little sore? We had to lock the office door for a week to make sure nobody came in and shot us all in the head. The rage kindled by the acquittal made us the most hated magazine in America. The New York office had to disconnect its toll-free number because the outraged calls they were getting overburdened the system.

For weeks afterward, we hated having to pick up the phone because it was nothing but endless aggravation and abuse. "I hope you have children, raise them to be tall and strong, and love them with all your heart. And then I hope you have to watch as someone slices them to pieces in front of your eyes," one little old lady yelled at me.

At the end of the whole ordeal, the entire landscape of American journalism had been changed forever, to say nothing of the social and legal upheaval that will continue for years.

"Real" news reporters had to scrounge through the pages of the tabloids for news tidbits. Viewers had grown accustomed to hearing stories reported in the finest tabloid style, built around a kernel of fact and surrounded by a nebulous cloud of rumor, assumption, and hype. In the fallout of the Simpson case, whatever line was once there that separated tabloid news from "real" news simply isn't there anymore.

AFTERWORD

The immunity journalists had in the early seventies no longer exists. If you call somebody a thieving pigfucker now, you'd better be ready to produce the pig.

—Dr. Hunter S. Thompson

I f a tabloid prints that sort of thing, it's smut," noted New York Times *owner Adolph Ochs, "but when the* New York Times *prints it, it's a sociological study." With this statement, Ochs pretty much cut to the heart of the debate over tabloid news. Of course, he also revealed the fundamental hypocrisy at work among the so-called legitimate press, who cling to their paper-thin illusion of clean hands and pure motives.*

When I began working for the Star *in 1989, tabloid news was belittled at every turn. I can't tell you how many times I had to explain that I didn't do Bigfoot/Alien Abduction/ Elvis Lives stories.*

In the seven years of my career, journalists who had previously turned up their noses at tabloid news have come begging for help. It is with mixed feelings that I have observed the mass media migration to my neighborhood, to Tabloidland. It's kinda' fun to see them struggle with their initial squeamishness, to have to hunker down and rake the muck for soiled gems, just as I did. But on the other hand, I've been a little disappointed. I had hoped that there might be something to aspire to someday.

205

Even before the O.J. Simpson trial, the mainstream press had started to hang around tabloid reporters enough to get the juicy stuff. Then they would preface their stories by saying how awful those tabloid reporters are, and isn't this all so ludicrous, and by the way, here's the dirt you've been lusting after. It's a really disingenuous way of keeping your hands clean.

Which brings us to the heart of the tabloid industry and the crux of this book.

Tabloid news sells.

In the late 1980s, the United States was in the midst of a debt-fueled euphoria, and the top paper in the country was the Wall Street Journal. *Whoever said that "imitation is the sincerest form of flattery" never met newly minted news executives desperate to show the bottom line to their corporate masters. The push was on to expand business pages, make them bigger and better, reap the benefits of the go-go eighties.*

Later, the number one paper in the country was USA Today. *That was about the same time your local daily started running color photos and garish pictographs on its front page, "packaging" stories and graphics, and reducing the length of stories to accommodate the shorter attention spans of the TV generation.*

Today the latest gimmick to get the audience to tune in is to serve up hot, juicy tabloid news. It's all because the people running newspapers and TV stations make their decisions based on the most trendy of evils: the marketing focus group. The marketers, with their degrees in statistical analysis, round up the usual suspects who conform to demographic profiles. They show the group a bunch of alternative front pages with different stories played up or down, with various arrangements of photos and artwork, and see which one gets the best response. There is very little thought given to what is the most important story, or which story will best serve the reader or viewer and society in general.

*I am convinced that if the marketing people came in to-
morrow with a report saying that pictures of live puppies
being fed into a meat grinder would boost sales 100 percent, we'd see a four-part series on this exciting new sport.
Lavishly illustrated, of course, with charts and pie graphs
to tell the numbers behind the story.*

*There are no regulatory agencies that make sure the
media meet certain standards. Nor should there be. But letting profit dictate ethics is a treacherous and short-sighted
policy, especially when the media's influence is as perva-
sive and powerful as it is in our plugged-in society. Every
study shows that newspapers and TV stations increase their
audience whenever they sensationalize the news. The best
example of this is in the coverage of crime: "If it bleeds, it
leads."*

*Relentless special exposés create a crime-centered cul-
ture in which people think crime is a much more serious
problem than it really is. Check the facts. Contrary to every
hair-raising newscast and prime-time real-life cop show,
crime is actually on the decline. But with the instantaneous
capabilities of satellite TV (freeway chase, anyone?), crimes
that normally would have been relegated to the back page
are now drilled into the national consciousness. Especially
if there's good video.*

*As a result, Americans have become frightened and are
buying guns, barricading themselves in their homes, moving out of the inner city, and voting for big bond proposi-
tions to build more jails.*

*The perception becomes the reality, and like a magic
funhouse mirror, the press distorts society, which then
morphs itself to fit to that twisted image. As gonzo journalist Hunter S. Thompson said, "You'd better be ready to produce the pig."*

*Well, that's the job of the media these days. Our job is to
produce the pig, hold it up for all to see, and give it its fifteen minutes of fame, a cover story, and a guest shot on
Leno. We produce the pig because you demand it. You want*

to hear the pig's side of the story, live, nationwide, in 3-D if possible.

And as long as you keep buying, someone will always be there to keep selling.

And someone like me will still be sitting in a car, drinking bad coffee, and getting paid to produce the pig.

David LaFontaine
Los Angeles, California